"Did Max put you up to it?" Carl's voice was sharp

"It's entirely the sort of thing he would do. Like getting you into my film. He's killing two birds with one stone. Hindering me, and giving you what you want."

Eve's temper rose. "It's never been my intention to act, but Max wants me to, and..." She stopped at the look of derision on his face.

"Don't take me for a fool, Eve. Max has already told me what this means to you so let's cut out the protestations of innocence. You may rule Max, but to me you're nothing special. I don't intend to smooth your path for you. You'll work as you've never worked before. Got it?"

How was it possible, Eve wondered, to still be attracted to him? To be attracted to someone who treated you with contempt was pure masochism.

AMANDA BROWNING is a new British author who lives in Essex. She is single, and a former librarian. Her lively contemporary writing style appeals to readers everywhere.

Books by Amanda Browning

HARLEQUIN PRESENTS
1055—PERFECT STRANGERS

HARLEQUIN ROMANCE
3031—THE ASKING PRICE

AMANDA BROWNING

web of deceit

Harlequin Books

TORONTO • NEW YORK • LONDON
AMSTERDAM • PARIS • SYDNEY • HAMBURG
STOCKHOLM • ATHENS • TOKYO • MILAN

Harlequin Presents first edition January 1991
ISBN 0-373-11329-3

Original hardcover edition published in 1990
by Mills & Boon Limited

CHAPTER ONE

THE chauffeur held the door for Eve to climb into the Rolls. She did so with a brief word of thanks, still uncomfortable with these marked trappings of a lifestyle poles apart from her own upbringing. Sinking back into the seat, she forced herself to relax as Max took his place beside her. The door closed, and the driver swiftly slipped in behind the wheel and set the car in motion. They swept down the gracious curve of the drive and out on to the highway.

Eve sensed Max move beside her, and then soundlessly the partition rose to cut them off from the man in the front seat. She tensed immediately, knowing that if Max wanted privacy it could only be for something she wouldn't like. She waited in silence for what would happen next.

At her side, Max Nilsson gave a small sigh of satisfaction, 'You're looking particularly lovely this evening, my dear.'

Eve moistened dry lips and sent a flickering glance his way. 'Thank you.'

Max laughed, the sound as silky and deadly as a cobra. 'Always so cool, Eve. That's what I like about you the most. All that fire locked up in ice. A fascinating combination. Added to beauty and intelligence, it is irresistible. You are a very lucky woman.'

She flinched, a fact he acknowledged with a smile. 'I don't happen to think so,' she returned flatly.

Max picked up her left hand, studying the slim, elegant fingers with appreciation. 'But you should. Your looks are your most valuable asset, my dear. Without them...' He paused, feeling the tension communicated through her hand. He patted it soothingly. 'Well, we

5

both know what would have happened without them, so I'll say no more.'

The knot in Eve's stomach tightened. He had no need to remind her that by rights she could be serving a prison sentence for embezzlement. He did it because he enjoyed reminding her of her position, and of what he could, and would, do if she refused to co-operate.

'I have a present for you, Eve.' Max's body came in contact with hers briefly as he moved to reach into the pocket of his jacket and extract a long, narrow box.

Eve's stomach cramped as she recognised the unmistakable mark of the jeweller. Max flicked the catch with his thumb and raised the lid on the ice-cold contents.

'I saw them and immediately thought of you, my dear Eve. The fire of ice, that burns with its beauty.'

She knew better than to move away or even flinch as he deftly fastened the diamond bracelet about her wrist and held it up to let the light spark off the facets. She could feel him waiting. She would have to find something to say, some lie that would satisfy his ego.

'They're very lovely,' she murmured tautly, and looked away from them before she shuddered. As her eyes rose, they met the knowing ones of the chauffeur in the rear-view mirror. Disgust rose to choke her as she lifted her chin and stared him out. Let him think what he liked, she didn't care.

'There won't be a woman there to touch you, my dear,' Max declared softly, and, raising her hand, pressed a kiss to her palm.

Her eyes were drawn to his downbent head, the dark hair sprinkled liberally with grey. She felt as if it wasn't her hand at all, but someone else's, and she was watching from a million miles away.

'You know that's not true,' she dismissed the compliment frigidly.

Max straightened up, his grey eyes meeting hers confidently. 'There won't be a man there who doesn't wish he were in my shoes. But you'll show them you're mine, won't you, my dear?'

It wasn't a question but a command, and lowered lids hid her expression. 'Yes, Max, I'll show them I'm yours,' she agreed flatly.

At last he let her hand go, and it lay on her lap, the diamonds winking up at her. Eve stared bleakly out into the darkness. He had coveted her from the very first moment he'd seen her on that awful day back in London. She had never stood a chance. Once he had trapped her, he had taken her over completely, and she was helplessly caught in his toils.

'My dear, you're not listening.' Max's soft voice up-braided her, and, swallowing that constricting lump in her throat, she gave him all her attention.

For the remainder of the journey, she sat in silence, listening to Max's scathing commentary on the guests they would meet at the party tonight. He had a vicious tongue and a spiteful nature. It showed in icy grey eyes and narrow mouth. She had good cause to know how ruthless he was too. Yet, he was held in awe in the world of high finance, as a man who knew how to make a shrewd buck. His nature didn't win friends, but then he didn't seek them. He lived and breathed power. No one got away from him once they made the mistake of underestimating him. She knew that only too well.

The car came to a smooth halt before one of Massachusetts' most imposing mansions, and the chauffeur came round to hold the door for them to alight. She paused while Max adjusted the mink coat about her shoulders. It wasn't a cold evening, but then, that wasn't the point of the exercise. With his hand clasped firmly about her arm, they mounted the steps to the porticoed entrance, and were admitted.

Eve had been to numerous functions just like this since meeting Max, and she didn't expect to enjoy it any more than she had the others. With a sigh of relief, she left him in the hall while she mounted the stairs to the second floor, yet from past experience she knew that Max would still be there, no matter how long she took to come back down. He guarded her jealously, and she hated it.

There were a few women in the bedroom when she walked in, and she recognised them all. They returned her greeting coolly, then proceeded to ignore her. Eve shrugged her shoulders. She was used to it by now. She tossed the mink carelessly on to the bed and, turning to the mirror, checked her appearance swiftly.

What she saw reflected there wasn't the Eve Hunter she knew. The black designer dress clung lovingly to every curve, outlining her long legs and lovely line of hip into a narrow waist. The strapless bodice only served to emphasise the ripe swell of her breasts. Diamonds glittered at her throat and ears. Max didn't like loose hair, so her platinum locks were swept up into a graceful style that drew attention to the vulnerable curve of her nape.

Eve didn't recognise the face, although she knew every feature intimately: the generous tilt of her lips, the high cheekbones and fine skin. Nor did she recognise the eyes. She couldn't look for long at the large violet eyes with their frame of long lashes, for she couldn't bear to see the truth reflected there.

Abruptly she turned her back and left the room. Max was still where she had left him, one eye on the stairs even as he talked with two men she didn't recognise. He saw her and, interpreting his look, Eve made her way towards them, all too aware of the way three pairs of eyes clung to every sway of her hips as she walked. There was a rebellious flush to her cheeks as she came to a halt, staring the two men out until it was they who looked away first.

Max's hand caressed her shoulder-blades and came to rest on her shoulder. 'My dear, let me introduce you to two old friends of mine, Josh Kennet and Walt Bachmann. We have some business to discuss, and I don't want to trouble your beautiful little head with it.

You can run along and enjoy the party. I'll try not to be too long, my dear. I'll make it up to you later.'

Flushing, Eve turned away, hating Max for that degrading dismissal. Behind her, ribald male laughter broke out, and she knew that she was the butt of the joke. Her colour died, leaving her cheeks pale with humiliation. Sensitive to the atmosphere, she knew she was the topic of conversation in more than one group that she passed, and felt their eyes like a scourge.

She halted on the edge of the vast drawing-room. Enjoy the party, Max had declared, knowing that she couldn't. Her eyes scanned the laughing, chattering groups of Massachusetts' finest society, seeing the male speculation and female contempt. The open looks and pointed comments she was meant to notice. She had been introduced to them all, but she was only tolerated because of Max. Without him, they had no hesitation in shunning her.

Eve lifted her chin. She might not like these people, but she could be wounded by their lack of human kindness. One thing she did know, she would never let them know they drew blood! She took a glass from a passing waiter and lifted it to the nearest group, who were staring with open rudeness. She smiled grimly as they turned away at once. Score one to her.

As she turned away, she was caught on the end of a dark blue gaze. Her startled eyes took in the height and breadth of the man. Over six feet of lean, powerful masculinity. He had a shock of dark hair atop a ruggedly handsome face that had strength and authority stamped on it. Yet his mouth was beautifully moulded, the lips showing a softer, more passionate side. Incredibly, he was casually dressed in a grey lounge suit, his white silk shirt tieless and open at the neck. He stood alone, to one side. Non-conforming in a society where conformity was the backbone.

She saw all this in seconds, saw too the approving inclination of his head, and the laughter on his lips as he raised his glass to her in silent salute.

Finding an ally in the enemy camp lightened her heart, and she laughed softly. Eyes dancing, she returned the salute, sipping at her own drink. Then people moved, blocking him from sight, and she sighed wistfully, setting her lips firmly before turning away. Slowly she followed the sound of music to the ballroom. Standing on the outskirts, she watched the glittering couples dance by. In the ordinary way she loved to dance, but Max only took her on the floor to show off his possession, and now the delight was tainted.

She sensed rather than saw someone come to stand at her side, and stiffened. On her own she was an open target for lone males, and being propositioned wasn't out of the question. Without exception, everyone wanted to sample Max's private supply. Tensely she awaited the first gambit.

'That's a hell of a sight. The privileged class enjoying its privileges!' a mocking voice drawled into her ear, and she looked round in surprise—right into the bluest pair of eyes she had ever seen. They belonged, unquestionably, to her erstwhile ally.

Used to being either ignored or insulted, she found this something new. She couldn't help but smile. 'That's sacrilege!'

One fine eyebrow lifted, 'Don't tell me you're a subscriber?'

Her eyes went back to the butterfly array and her mouth twisted, 'Hardly!'

'No,' he agreed softly, 'I thought not.'

There was a tone in his voice that brought her eyes to his questioningly. He grinned, and somehow managed to look both sexy and boyish. Eve's nerves tightened abruptly as her stomach lurched.

'It's pretty obvious why I'm unwelcome among my so-called peers. What makes you *persona non grata*?'

Eve's eyes widened in surprise. 'You must be a stranger here,' she stated drily.

'Ah!'

She met his look, expecting to see the familiar prurient interest, and saw only amusement.

'Meaning, I gather, that were I not I would know the why. What did you do, seduce the vicar?' he queried sardonically.

Surprised into laughter, Eve shook her head.

'Worse than that?' he probed, blue eyes dancing.

For the first time ever, her situation seemed funny. 'Don't ask!' she advised wryly.

'Interesting,' he declared thoughtfully, eyes intent on the curve of her lips and the way her eyes crinkled up as she laughed. Then his gaze drifted over her shoulder and he frowned. 'We seem to be attracting a great deal of attention.'

Eve looked around too, having forgotten that they were not alone. He was right. There were enough eyes on them to outfit the Hydra, and most of them malicious. Yet strangely, with this man so close, it was as if nothing could reach her tonight. In some indefinable way he had brought down a magnetic field about them that shielded her. Her heart stepped up its tempo as she grinned.

'Talking to me for too long will ruin your reputation,' she advised lightly.

He looked amused and intrigued. 'Is that so? You must be some sort of unholy terror. Am I to assume you eat men like me for breakfast?'

She laughed because he made it sound so absurd, yet she felt compelled to say, 'No, really. For your own good, you should go.' She meant it. She liked this stranger, and, by the skittering of her nerves, knew she could so easily like him too much. Which was impossible. This was no fairy-story, and she was no Cinderella. Though she didn't want him to go, her conscience told her to be honest with him.

What he did was to shake his head and reach out to remove the glass from her fingers and set it aside. 'I'll take my chances. Besides, it's only fair you should know that my reputation was ruined a long time ago.' He grinned down at her roguishly and Eve suddenly found it difficult to breathe. Her reply was breathy.

'Now that I can believe. What did you do?'

He leant forward and his answer was for her ears only. She gasped, choked, and burst into a delightful gurgle of laughter that drew all eyes.

'So, now you know,' he declared, eyes twinkling in response to her enjoyment.

Yes, she knew, but she didn't believe it for a second. He probably thought she was joking too. But she wasn't and she couldn't let him go on thinking it. She strove to keep her voice light. 'It's only fair that I should tell you my secret too.'

'Fair, perhaps, but unnecessary.'

Her lips parted. 'You . . . don't want to know?'

'I'm really not interested in true confessions. I very much doubt that anything this crowd found damning would scandalise me. First impressions are usually the most accurate ones, and I've always been a strong believer in using my own judgement,' he told her in all seriousness, though he was smiling.

Eve felt shaky, and more than a little bemused as she stared up at him. 'And what does your judgement tell you about me?' The question popped out before she could stop it.

'That you're someone I'd like to get to know better. Shall we dance? They seem to be playing our song.'

'Our song?' Somewhere her wits had gone begging.

He smiled right down into her eyes. '"Strangers in the night". Corny, perhaps, but who knows? So, what do you say, shall we take a chance?'

Maybe it was stupid. She was certain to regret it later, but there was something about him that she couldn't fight. 'I'd love to dance,' she agreed huskily, and, uncaring of everyone and everything, allowed him to lead her out on to the dance-floor and into his arms.

They moved together so smoothly that they could have done this a thousand times, so well did they fit together. Eve felt the strong arms close about her, heard the deep thud of his heart beneath her ear, and gave herself up to a heady enjoyment. She knew she was flying in the face of danger, but she couldn't give this moment up. Something was happening to her tonight, something magical. In this man's arms she felt all her troubles disappear, and she wanted that security to go on and on.

'What brought you here if this is how they treat you?' His voice was a low, husky drawl in her ear that sent shivers down her spine.

Eve closed her eyes. There should have been more time! Yet wasn't it only right that it should be he who brought reality back? 'I...came with someone,' she said shortly, and felt the arms about her tense.

'I see.' The words were flat acceptance of her statement.

She swallowed against a growing lump in her throat. 'I should have told you.'

He didn't deny it. 'Are you going to leave with him?'

She licked her lips. 'Yes.' Was he angry? He had a right to be. Lord, she was such a fool!

'Are you married, or otherwise involved?' came the next soft question.

He didn't sound angry at all. 'Otherwise involved,' Eve admitted huskily, then lost her breath as for an instant it felt as if his cheek brushed her hair. But that couldn't be, for in the next second he was easing her away to arm's length, leaving her feeling chilled and abandoned.

He was smiling ruefully, but his eyes were shaded. 'Just my luck. When I find you, you're already spoken for,' he teased, but there was a distance now that had been missing before. 'What happened? Did you argue?'

How foolish to feel so lost! 'Not exactly; he's talking business.'

'He'd do better to abandon business for one night and protect you from these vultures instead.' There was a note of steel in the joking comment.

Her smile was crooked. 'I'll tell him,' she promised, trying to keep just the right note.

'Do that,' he advised, just as the music ended. For a second they were left facing each other, islanded amid a sea of chattering partygoers. Then his hand under her elbow urged her to the side.

Eve took a deep breath and smiled apologetically. 'I'm sorry if I gave you the wrong impression, I——'

'One dance isn't a sin, and I happened to enjoy this one, very much. As I said, it was just bad luck,' he declared with a shrug.

'Yes.' What else could she do but agree?

The stranger—she still didn't know his name, and now it was pointless to ask—sighed and stuffed his hands into his trouser pockets. 'Do you want me to help you find him?'

Alarm bells pealed. 'That wouldn't be wise,' she evaded softly.

'The jealous type?'

At least she could be honest here. 'Very.'

He stared down at her ruefully. 'It's a damn shame. He's a lucky guy.'

Eve almost laughed and spoilt it all. 'He thinks so,' she said evenly, feeling a weight of desolation settle about her shoulders. 'It wasn't our song after all, but perhaps another time we could dance to it, just for old time's sake?' she offered, but he shook his head.

'I make it a rule never to poach on another man's preserve.'

She knew that instinctively, and yet... 'Tonight——'

'Was a mistake,' he interrupted shortly, then smiled. 'An enjoyable one, but a mistake none the less.'

She knew who had made it, too. 'You're very generous, when it was all my fault.'

He laughed lightly. 'Your mountain is a molehill. You were angry, I was available. We flirted. It sounds like a French exercise. The truth is that nothing happened, nobody got hurt. We'll both know better next time.'

'Then you aren't angry?'

He reached out a finger and gently traced the line of her cheek. 'Only with myself for being too late. If I were the cad some people think me, I'd say to hell with him, whoever he is, but I'm not. So I'll accept my defeat graciously. Now, chin up! Don't let them grind you down. And I'd better go and get myself a drink before I say something that would be better left unsaid.' That finger brushed over her lips once before he smiled wryly and, turning, vanished into the crowd.

Eve stared blankly after him, feeling as if a vital part of her was irretrievably lost. She shivered and became aware at once that she was the centre of attention. The talk and looks were avid, and suddenly it proved too much. She kept her chin up as she backtracked to the hall in full retreat. Her only desire was to be alone, and she found that sanctuary in the upstairs bathroom.

Locking the door, she sank down on to the edge of the bath. For a moment in time she had been special to someone. She knew that as she knew day followed night. She didn't know who he was, but it didn't matter. For a while she had felt alive. It had been exhilarating— wonderful. A brightness in her darkest hours.

Only now she began to shake as she realised what a risk she had run in indulging herself that way. But luck had been on her side. Max didn't know. She doubted if he ever would. But even if he did, she couldn't regret those moments when a kind of magic had entered her life in the guise of a blue-eyed, dark-haired man. She would never see him again, but she would never forget him.

She sighed and pulled herself together. He had gone. She had sent him away because she had no choice. She was committed to Max. There wasn't room for—hopeless dreams. Yet she smiled to herself, because he had gone knowing her only as a woman he had been attracted to, someone he liked, and now someone out there knew what she was really like. Reality was suddenly a little more bearable for that.

Eve checked her make-up, seeing the flush on her cheeks and the glitter in her eyes. There was nothing she could do about it. All she could hope was that Max wouldn't notice. Her heart quailed a little as she realised that by now any one of a number of people could have been only too happy to tell Max of her dance with the stranger. But there was nothing she could do about that either, except face it if and when she had to. So, setting her shoulders, she made her way downstairs again.

Max was in the hall, clearly waiting for her. One look at his face told her he wasn't best pleased. The grip he took on her arm underlined it. She paled a little, but refused to be intimidated.

'What have you been up to, Eve?' he asked, grey eyes nailing her to the spot.

'Up to?' she queried evenly, but her mind jolted violently. Oh, God, what did he know?

'Someone said they thought they saw you running this way,' he stated, watching her closely.

Eve breathed again. Someone had been stirring, but hadn't been brave enough to come right out with it. She kept her cool. 'I never run anywhere, Max, but I did hurry. I thought I had stained my dress and I went upstairs to fix it. That was all.' The lie tripped smoothly off her tongue.

Eyes like gimlets, Max tested that for a nerve-racking second before his grip eased. He smiled. 'That had better be all, my dear. Now, come along, there's someone I want you to meet.'

He slipped his arm about her waist, his hand resting possessively on her hip. For a brief moment Eve shut her eyes, relief battling with the horror that always threatened on these occasions. Then she heard the shutters go down in her head, shutting off all feeling, allowing her to go forward and feel nothing. They passed from group to group, Max always a little distracted as he searched the crowded rooms. Finally the hand on her hip tightened fractionally, and she knew that he had spied his quarry, and something more. This meeting was very important to him. He was almost on a high with suppressed emotion.

Eve moved obediently to the pressure. At first she couldn't see whom he was making for, then the crowd shifted, and she saw it was for one group by the door on to the terrace. She braced herself for this meeting, knowing there would be the usual male ribaldry. The salacious looks and whispered asides.

'Carl.'

At the sound of the name, the group parted, leaving Eve staring straight into the eyes of her stranger. Her lips parted on a silent gasp of shock. She saw the instant recognition on his face, the pleasure, then his gaze flickered from her to Max. Her throat closed over at the shocked disbelief she saw in his eyes as he stiffened, followed by the shutters going down. Slowly his eyes returned to her and she blanched at the cold contempt there. Her free hand clutched at her stomach, for it felt as if the bottom had just fallen out of her world.

'My dear, let me introduce you to Carl Ramsay. Carl, this is the young lady we discussed, Eve Hunter.'

At the sound of Max's voice, she jumped, desperately gathering her scattered composure. 'Mr Ramsay,' she greeted gruffly.

Dear God, his eyes were full of a cold, bitter anger, and deep revulsion. She couldn't believe it—didn't want to. But it was in the chilly wastes of his voice too, as he said with insolent mockery, 'You're to be congratulated,

Max. It appears you've found your…paradise.' He lifted
the glass he held in salute.

Eve winced at the derision, but Max laughed, his hand
caressing the subtle curve of her hip. Blue eyes followed
the movement and those beautiful lips curled.

'Why, thank you, Carl. I've been telling Eve so for
months, but she refuses to believe me.'

The man she now knew as Carl Ramsay gave a harsh
bark of laughter that made her shudder. 'Modesty be-
comes a woman. Especially one so very lovely.'

It wasn't a compliment and they both knew it. Hurt
turned her violet eyes to black. She could feel Max's
impatience beside her and knew she must say something
quickly. 'You flatter me, Mr Ramsay,' she uttered
hoarsely.

Carl laughed again and downed the rest of his drink.
'On the contrary,' he disagreed smoothly, 'Max has
found a pearl among pearls.'

She was shocked by his open disparagement before
Max, but even more so, when she cast a searching look
at the man by her side, to see the gleam of pleasure in
his eyes. It dawned on her sickeningly that these two
men were old sparring partners, who knew each other
very well, and had a mutual loathing. That loathing was
now transferred to her by association. Her blood ran
cold. It was more than that. He now knew who and what
she was. She saw the knowledge in his eyes. Suddenly
all he knew of her from those earlier moments ceased
to exist. She had thought he was different, but he was
the same as the rest. She battled with a devastating sense
of loss, locking away her own fragile feelings in ice. He
wasn't worth a tear. Bitterness lay thick in her throat.

'Then you'll admit I was right? She'll be perfect,' Max
was urging as Eve dragged herself from the black pit of
her thoughts.

Carl inclined his head. 'I have to agree that she looks
right. You drive a shrewd bargain, Max. I trust

her…talents…match her looks.' The pause wasn't subtle, but Max merely chuckled.

'They do. I'm not very often mistaken.'

Eve felt soiled, and wanted to scream when those eyes ran over her again. 'In that case we'll both be happy. Until the weekend, then, Max.'

He moved away with barely a nod for Eve. She stared after him, chilled by a sense of betrayal and abandonment. Sluggishly her brain recalled what had been said, and for a reason she couldn't explain she felt a sudden desperation as she turned to Max. It took all her ability to keep her voice level.

'What did he mean? What were you talking about?'

Max smiled broadly. 'That, my dear, is a surprise that I intend to keep until later. However, it does call for a drink.'

He turned in search of a waiter, and as he did so Eve couldn't stop her eyes from straying to where Carl Ramsay stood. She looked straight into the full force of those incredible eyes and the full weight of his contempt. It was a shrivelling, blunt-edged weapon, and inside her something screamed. She was transfixed, unable to move her eyes away, and her face froze in rigour. Only pride kept her from collapsing in a quivering heap where she stood. Pride and a knowledge that he had no right to judge her.

'My dear.'

Max's voice made her start, but it broke that dreadful contact. She blinked, and when she looked again Carl Ramsay had disappeared. She turned to face Max with less than her usual grace, and he picked it up immediately.

'What's wrong?'

Now Eve found herself facing his narrowed grey eyes, and felt, hysterically, as if she were surrounded by eyes of all shades. She called on all her powers of invention to hide the truth because, if he knew, how he would laugh. How he would enjoy using her foolishness against her! She raised a fluttering hand to her temple. 'I . . . feel a little faint, Max. Is it hot in here?'

'A little, perhaps,' he agreed, narrowed eyes never leaving her pale face.

She licked her lips. 'If you don't mind, I think I'll step outside for a moment. I need some fresh air.'

She could have screamed when, as usual, Max debated that for a second or two before agreeing. 'Very well, my dear, but don't stay away too long. You know how I dislike being parted from you.'

Resisting the urge to run as if hounded, Eve made good her escape. The air outside was blessedly cool, the terrace deserted. She was glad, because she wanted peace, to be alone with this latest defeat. Noise bubbled out behind her, urging her footsteps on towards the camouflaging darkness of the shadows at the end. She went as far as she could go until the wall stopped her. Her fingers curled over the stonework as she took deep, cleansing lungfuls of the delicately scented air. Dear lord, it felt so good!

Overhead a cloud passed across the moon on its way out to sea. How she wished it would swoop down and carry her off—away from the soul-destroying life she led. The sky was such an intense, deep blue, it reminded her of a pair of eyes. Oh, God! Don't think about it! Don't let him tear you apart because he has let you down. He was nothing to you, as you were clearly nothing to him!

'You know, I would have thought that any woman would find it degrading to be pawed in public,' a husky voice floated out to her from the darkness.

Her heart lurched as she recognised those now scornful tones. Every nerve in her body was tensed as she stiffened and turned to seek him out. Carl Ramsay's face was a paler shadow in the darkness surrounding them. She could feel his contempt like a tangible ghost. Yet strangely she was thankful for it. He had reminded her where her commitments lay. Whatever he thought, however it made her feel, her loyalty must be to Max. And more. She would not let him see just how much of a blow his defection had been, for she had her pride.

She lifted her chin a fraction. 'We all have differing tastes, Mr Ramsay.' Was that really her voice sounding so cool and disdainful?

'So, it pleases you to be treated like a whore off the streets, does it? To know that Max gets his kicks from watching every man want you? Was that the purpose of that little come-on earlier?' Disgust dripped from every horrible word.

Eve shuddered, then controlled it swiftly. Lord, how easily his arrows evaded her armour and struck home. She lifted one shoulder carelessly and half turned back to the view of the elegant lawns. That 'come-on', as he'd called it, had been nothing of the sort, but she wasn't going to argue.

'It's no big thing.' The lie choked her, for it was torture. It crucified her.

'You sell yourself cheaply, darling.'

Angry tears sprang into her eyes, making the night dance until she blinked them back and faced him, defiance in her raised chin and the set of her smile. 'I know my worth, Mr Ramsay, down to the smallest groat.'

He was closer than she thought. His hand shot out to capture her left arm and raise it up before her face. 'And just how many groats did that cost, sweetheart?' he scorned, fingers biting into her flesh. 'Tiffany's?'

Her eyes flashed, 'Cartier's,' she returned, undaunted. He had no right to judge her. No man did. She tried to jerk her arm away, but he resisted.

'And what little service did you have to perform to get it? Or can I imagine?'

Her blood turned to ice in her veins as the insults cut deeper. How dared he? She had done nothing to deserve this condemnation. Hatred for him and his hypocrisy burst into life. 'I dare say you have an excellent imagination, Mr Ramsay, and I cannot stop you indulging it. Now I'll thank you to let me go.' She used every ounce of her control to make her voice equally cold.

He let her go with unflattering speed, as if her touch defiled him. 'My, how you've changed,' he jeered. 'Half an hour ago all pliant femininity, and now as hard as nails. Well, I trust the diamonds are adequate compensation for being an old man's mistress. Max is sixty, if he's a day. You couldn't be more than twenty-one.'

If she had changed, it was no more than he, and with more cause! No man had ever said the things this man was saying, and every word drew blood. She hated him for that. 'I'm twenty-four, if it's any of your business. And just why are you so angry? Can you be envious, Mr Ramsay?' she taunted recklessly.

His laughter made her want to curl up and die. 'Darling, I wouldn't have you if you came gift-wrapped. I'd never take Max's leavings!'

Her gasp was audible, anger making her rash. 'That isn't what you were saying before. You were definitely interested then!' she reminded him goadingly.

His smile wasn't pleasant. 'And you were tempted.' He laughed when her head went back. 'I'm not blind. You were all dewy eyes and trembling lips. You almost had me hooked. Now I realise you were just a predatory female trawling for fresh meat. I had a lucky escape, but why? Why did you get cold feet? Could it be my outer trappings that put you off? Did you remember just how much money Max is worth? It's fortunate you didn't know who I was, because by now I'd probably be stuck with you. For future reference, Miss Hunter, my personal fortune exceeds Max's by several million dollars. You could have been on to a good thing, but you blew it.'

Eve was starting to shake with a mounting anger. 'Then I'm glad I did, for Max is infinitely preferable to a conceited ape like you. At least he's generous. I get everything I want. In fact, I don't even have to ask for it. So even if you were to ask me, I would never leave Max. Do you hear me? Never!'

There was a deathly silence in which the only sound was angry breathing. Then Carl Ramsay broke it with a contemptuous laugh. 'You and Max deserve one another. I'll remember that. As for the rest, God help us all! Max might enjoy playing William Randolph Hearst, but in my book, you're no Marion Davies. At least she had talent.'

'Goodnight, Mr Ramsay. I'd say it was a pleasure meeting you, but I'd be lying,' she said quellingly.

'Another talent?' he mocked back.

Not deigning to answer that, she walked away with her head high. She could feel his eyes boring into her back. How mistaken in him she had been! That brief interlude had been nothing but a practised ploy to get a woman for the night! And she had nearly fallen for it hook, line and sinker because she was so damned lonely. Well, she had had her eyes well and truly opened. She was going to have absolutely nothing to do with him after this.

As she stepped inside she forced him from her mind. Now she must find Max. She had been away far longer than she'd intended, thanks to that man, and he wouldn't like it. He would be angry, but she had weathered it before and would do so again. She found him in the midst of a group in one corner. When she joined him, he was all charm. Capturing her hand, he raised it to his lips.

'My dear, I missed you,' he declared softly, but there was nothing mild about the glitter in his eyes. 'Do you feel better?' he enquired solicitously.

What a joke, even spoken in anger, to declare she would never leave Max. One touch and she wanted to run in the other direction. 'Much better. I knew the air would do me good. May I have a drink?' She needed it desperately.

'Of course, my dear. How remiss of me.' He patted her hand and signalled to a waiter.

From where she was standing, Eve had a good view of Carl Ramsay coming in from the terrace. He looked her way and saw the hold Max had on her. Eve lifted her chin as he gave her one all-encompassing look of contempt before walking away. Shivering, she had to stop herself from downing the drink Max held out to her in one desperate go.

CHAPTER TWO

'WHAT kept you so long, my dear?' Max's voice was deceptively mild.

It was after midnight, and they were in the car on the way home, the glass partition sealing them into their private cocoon. The intervening hours had been a test of her nerve, because revealing nothing of what she was feeling to Max was her priority. She was drained by the time they left, but she knew it wasn't over. She had known the inquisition would start as soon as they were alone. Now she had to be very careful.

'I didn't realise I was so long. I'm sorry,' she apologised in a placatory monotone.

'Who did you talk to?' he probed gently, insistently, holding her hand in his.

Eve willed her rioting nerves not to flinch. 'What makes you think I was talking to someone?' His jealousy and possessiveness were the usual aftermath to any outing and always left her feeling sick inside, but now there was an added menace.

There was a moment's pause. 'Eve, my dear, I've told you before, I won't have you lying to me. You're young and beautiful, but there are other young and beautiful women. You are dispensable. If you're lying to me, you have until we get home to change your mind.'

Eve was careful not to move or make any sign that she was alarmed by the threat, but her brain began to whirl. Had someone told him? Had he seen her out on the terrace with Carl Ramsay? She didn't want to admit to that awful conversation they had had. If she did, Max would extract every detail, and that would mean him learning of her earlier encounter with Carl. So was he testing her? He had done it before, psyched her into admitting something he didn't know. He could be doing it now. She must decide what the odds were. He loved these mind games, thrived on them. Had he seen her or hadn't he? There wasn't much time to decide to bluff the bluffer.

The car came to a smooth halt. Max helped her out and escorted her into the elegant hall where a lamp glowed softly. He was at her heels as they mounted the stairs, a constant reminder that their conversation was unfinished. Eve let herself into her room and flicked on the light. Max followed her, shutting the door behind him. She tossed her bag on to the bed and the mink followed it. Taking a deep breath, she faced him once more with all the cool at her disposal.

'Well, Eve?' He walked towards her, looking charming and distinguished with his overcoat undone, the silk scarf draped about his neck.

'I haven't lied to you, Max,' she stated firmly.

Slowly his hands came out to run up her arms and across her shoulders, coming to rest on her throat. He stopped like that for a moment, leaving her wondering just what was coming next, then he smiled.

'Good.' His fingers urged her closer. 'You're mine, Eve, remember that.'

His mouth came down on hers in a kiss that was totally possessive. Eve stared unblinking at the wall, allowing him to do as he pleased, yet by her side her nails carved arcs into her palms. Finally he released her and stepped back.

'Always so cool, so submissive. You'd do anything for your freedom, wouldn't you, Eve?'

Her lids flickered twice. 'You know I would,' she agreed heavily, resisting with an effort the urge to wipe her mouth.

Max smiled. 'Good, because I have a little job for you to do, my dear. Remember, I said that the time would come for you to pay off the debt? Shall we make ourselves comfortable?' He indicated the small sofa by the fireplace and they both sat down. Max crossed his legs and examined the toe of one highly polished shoe. 'What did you think of our Mr Ramsay?'

Eve didn't rush to answer. She bit down on the hot flood of hate that swept her, knowing that wasn't what he wanted to know. There was more to the idle question than met the eye. It was time for caution. 'He seemed...clever, confident.'

'Mmm. He's that and more. Much, much more. Carl Ramsay, my dear Eve, is a man with a mission. Such men are dangerous. He has something to prove. Something he thinks to get from me. Needless to say, he won't succeed, but it will make an interesting spectacle watching him being frustrated. I'm quite looking forward to it.

'But I'm digressing. Carl Ramsay, my dear Eve, is a *movie director*.' Max made it sound cheap, sleazy. 'At the present moment he is engaged on a television film about a family who used to live in this house. Naturally, he would like very much to use the original location, and I...' He paused, chuckling at some secret amusement. 'Why, I saw no reason why he shouldn't. Dear me, no. Upon conditions. I felt certain we could reach a...satisfactory agreement, and we have. I've given Carl Ramsay permission to use any part of the house he desires.' Here Max laughed again. 'And I'm sure he'll check out the attics and the cellars! As I say, that is his reward for agreeing to use you in one of the star parts.'

Eve very nearly missed the punchline, it was introduced so carelessly. When it registered she couldn't recall her gasp of shock. 'You can't be serious!'

'I've never been more so.'

Eve was horrified for two reasons, but having to work with Carl Ramsay paled beside the other. Her sense of justice revolted, irrespective of who was involved. 'But Max, I'm no actress. Wishing me on to him will be giving the film the kiss of death!' she protested.

Max beamed. 'Ah! I knew I could rely on you to ferret out the most salient point. My dear, you are in the film precisely to make sure it doesn't succeed.' He rubbed his hands. 'If Ramsay suspects it, he still won't refuse me.'

Eve froze at the malice in his voice, suddenly feeling ill. 'I don't understand.' She knew the two men were enemies, but this was unbelievable.

'It's really very simple. I want the film to flop. You will make sure it does so.'

There were things Max could make her do, but this wasn't one of them. Hurting other people, even Carl Ramsay, was not on. 'I won't do it.'

Max raised one eyebrow. 'I hope very much that you will change your mind, my dear,' he said softly.

That tone was a threat in itself, but she shivered and ignored it. 'Never. I won't be made a party to such a thing.'

'Coming from you, my dear Eve, moral scruples seem a little . . . hypocritical.' He sighed heavily and rose to his feet. Eve watched with an anxiously beating heart as he crossed to her bedside table and lifted the telephone receiver. Slowly, he began to dial. She stood up quickly.

'What are you doing?'

He paused, finger poised over the next digit. 'I'm calling my lawyer to instruct him to instigate proceedings for embezzlement against one Eve Hunter, my dear. The resulting scandal will be unavoidable, but these things happen.'

Eve couldn't move as she watched the dial spin round. Then suddenly movement returned and she was by his side, hand coming down firmly to cut the call off. 'No!'

'No? But you just told me——'

'I changed my mind,' she declared raggedly, breathing very fast.

Max put the receiver back on its rest. 'Ah, one of woman's most admirable prerogatives. Now, to get back to our Mr Ramsay. You will take that part in his film and do your utmost to make it fail. Is that understood?'

Eve closed her eyes for a second, then nodded. 'Yes, I understand. Why are you doing this, Max?'

He patted her cheek. 'That, my dear, is my business. All you have to remember is that by doing this for me you remain free. Now, the arrangements. Carl and his leading actors will be staying here with us. They will be arriving on Sunday, and the film unit on Monday, I believe. All arrangements for their comfort I shall leave in your capable hands. It's late now, so I'll wish you goodnight, my dear. Sleep well.'

She followed his departure with her eyes as he went through the door that joined their two rooms. As the door clicked shut she collapsed weakly on to the edge of the bed, hands lifting to cover her face. What he was expecting her to do was disgusting, horrible—unavoidable. Damn him! He had her with her back to the wall. She had to do it, for there was more than her freedom at stake, much more.

Her hand stifled a hysterical laugh, for there was another aspect to this whole nightmare that even Max didn't suspect. She had lied to him when she'd said she wasn't an actress, for it was in her blood. Her mother had been the brilliant stage actress Colleen MacManus. That was the secret she still had to hide, and part of the horrendous chain of events which had led her into Max's clutches.

Colleen had married the sober, handsome young Gerald Hunter for love when she was just starting out in her career, and later he had let her go for the same reason. Strictly speaking, she should never have married nor had a child, for, to her, domesticity, however much she loved her family, was like taking a crystal into the shade to preserve its hues. All it did was fade away.

Gerald had known that, and let her go. Eve, watching his undying love for the glittering personality who was her mother, hadn't been able to understand or forgive the abandonment. So acting was bred in her, but was a talent she preferred to hide, unless forced to do it at school. She didn't want anything to do with it, for all she knew was that it wrecked lives and hurt people.

Then, when Eve was in her teens, Colleen came back. But it was a different woman from the one Eve remembered. For at the height of her powers and success Colleen had been struck down with a debilitating disease which would eventually kill her. From thinking her father foolish, observing her mother's silent courage and cheerfulness as the disease took hold, Eve finally came to terms with what the love her parents shared really was. Something that spanned time and distance and was unconquerable.

For a few years they were a family, but her mother's deterioration made her father decide to take her where she could get the best of care, and where he could stay with her. Eve was glad then that the world had been led to believe her mother had died years ago, for this sorrow was one that deserved to be kept private.

Only the sanatorium cost money. It was shocking how quickly her mother's wealth disappeared, and then her father's savings. Working herself, Eve helped all she could, and they had managed, up until some months ago when the money had run out. That was when Eve had a stroke of genius. She worked for the Nilsson Corporation in London. It seemed to her that if she approached Max Nilsson himself while he was in the country, it would be possible to arrange a personal loan. It wouldn't be unsecured either, for she would be coming in to an inheritance from her paternal grandmother when she was twenty-five, and that would more than cover the loan.

She hadn't liked Max at all when she went to see him, but her need was greater than her personal feelings, so she had pressed on with her request without saying more than was necessary. To her surprise, he hadn't even hesitated, but insisted that he saw no reason why it couldn't be arranged. She was to go ahead and advance herself the money without delay—an easy enough thing to do, for she worked in the loans department—and they would have an agreement drawn up.

How could she have known what he was like? She
couldn't have, but she soon found out. She arranged for
the money and sent it to her father, and waited for the
agreement to arrive. When it did, she signed it and returned it for Max's signature, then waited for her copy.
It never came. What did was the quarterly audit, which
found no trace of a loan, only that she had taken money
without authorisation. Embezzlement under any
circumstances.

Of course she explained, but who would believe her?
So she demanded to see Max Nilsson himself. He flew
over from America just to see her and, before witnesses,
stunned her by denying ever having made such an
agreement. In shock, she knew then that, for whatever
purpose he had, she had been well and truly trapped.
Alone, he offered her a choice: freedom if she went with
him, or prison, the latter involving a front-page scandal
that would not only reach her father, shocking him when
he was desperately worried about her mother, but would
also, inevitably, reveal that Colleen was still alive, if little
more than a helpless vegetable.

She had no choice, as he very well knew. He told her
he didn't want to know her secrets; what he wanted was
her, as his mistress. If her privacy meant so much, she
would agree without hesitation. Knowing that secrecy
was vital, she had done the only thing she could. Max
had been manipulating her ever since.

He had installed her in this mansion, this treasure-
house of antiques and *objets d'art*. She had become one
of his prized possessions, lavished with all the things a
woman could want. In the same way that he would look
at a favourite jade figurine, he would watch her, running
his hand caressingly over her smooth skin. From time
to time he even kissed her. Yet there was one thing the
rest of the world didn't know, and would never believe—Carl Ramsay more than most—he had never attempted to join her in her bed.

She was Max Nilsson's mistress in the eyes of the world, only he never touched her.

Initial relief was tempered by her growing knowledge of what this man was like. Then came the bargain. To all the world she was his mistress. Providing no one was allowed to guess the truth, her bed was her own. The reckoning would come later. For now she was flaunted as his mistress at every opportunity. Eve didn't know if he made no advance because he didn't want to, or because he couldn't. Not sleeping with him didn't lessen the shame or humiliation. She was a pawn to be used as he liked. That was what he enjoyed. The power he had over her every move.

Which was why he had known she would do her utmost to wreck Carl Ramsay's film.

She stood up abruptly and began to remove her jewellery with deliberate movements, casting it on to the dressing-table as if it were plastic beads. Unpinning her hair, she shook it loose. As she did so she caught sight of her reflection, and her eyes held their mirror image.

How ironic that, having avoided the stage for years because of her mother, she should now be embracing it to shield her. Ironic, but she wouldn't avoid it.

She thought of that tall, dark figure and shuddered. Her anger had died away in the light of events. She could never forgive what he had said, but now she understood a part of his contempt. Max had forced her on him and he despised her for it. If she were a vindictive person she would delight in carrying out Max's plans, but she wasn't. Hate Carl Ramsay though she did, she would hate her part more. Yet she had no choice. And if Carl found out? Dear lord, she would have no defence, for his anger would be entirely justified!

And while it all went on that master manipulator, Max, would be crowing with glee!

Unable to bear her own thoughts, she hurried through to the bathroom. Stripping off her clothes, she stepped beneath the stinging spray. Yet she knew that however much she scrubbed the outside of herself she would never feel clean on the inside again.

Carl Ramsay arrived alone on Sunday morning, driving himself up to the house in a shiny black sports car. Eve watched him from an upstairs window as he eased his long frame from the car. Today he was even more casually dressed in baggy white trousers and a pale blue silk shirt. He managed to look relaxed and powerful at the same time, and the wind-blown dark hair added a dash of rakishness. Put together, it was a very potent package.

He glanced up at the house as he shut the car door, and she wondered what he was thinking. It was an impressive structure in an area noted for them, with a tendency towards overdone Gothic revival. The grounds, though, would please even the most critical. Acres of lawns and woodland stretched down to the Atlantic shoreline. There were formal flower-beds and wild gardens. Tennis-courts, swimming-pool and stables dotted the area, never obtrusive. Everything was arranged in the best taste money could buy.

Somehow though, from his stance, he seemed more satisfied than impressed. His eyes ranged the lower floors meticulously, then lifted to the upper ones. Eve drew back instinctively, although she knew that at that distance he was unlikely to be able to see her. Even though he wore dark glasses, she felt the power of those penetrating eyes, and her nerves tensed, her heart beating a little faster.

She had failed to come to terms with what was expected of her during the interval since their last meeting. She would always be a reluctant participant. At the same time, she had remembered Max saying Carl knew he was being manipulated and accepted it. She couldn't understand why. There were other houses without strings attached, and who would know the difference? So he seemed to be entering the arena voluntarily, no lamb to the slaughter. Nothing about this was normal, and she shivered, her scalp prickling in alarm.

There wasn't time for more thought, because she saw Max come out on to the steps and hold out his hand. She couldn't hear what the two men said as they shook hands, but the gestures were friendly. And that was the greatest hypocrisy, for they weren't friends and never would be.

As they disappeared from view, Eve knew it was about time she made an appearance downstairs. Max would not be pleased if she showed any reluctance to play her part. She obeyed his orders implicitly, not because she was afraid, but because she was wary of what he might choose to do as a punishment. He had very subtle corrective measures.

The two men were still standing in the hall. Both looked up as she made her way down the elegant curving staircase. Eve was aware of Max's approval of her cream pencil skirt and white silk blouse with its deep neckline, yet it was Carl Ramsay who drew and held her unwilling attention. What *was* he thinking behind those dark glasses? Even as the thought came, he was whipping them off and she could see for herself. She needed no interpreter to translate that lancing contempt.

Her chin lifted as she stepped on to the highly polished floor and went to join them, the embers of her anger bursting into life again, fuelled by that look.

'Eve, my dear, come and greet our guest,' Max urged her.

It wasn't at all easy, under that watchful gaze, for Eve to slip her arm through Max's in a possessive gesture, but she managed and held out her hand. 'I'm pleased to meet you again, Mr Ramsay,' she greeted politely, only her eyes relaying entirely the opposite message.

For an awful moment she actually feared he was going to ignore her outstretched hand as he viewed her with one cynical eyebrow raised. The pause was just long enough to be eloquent before he remembered his manners and reached out to enfold her slim fingers in his much larger hand.

Their mutual antipathy was such that the charge that leapt between their touching palms was a shock. Startled, her eyes flew to his, and she knew he had felt it too by the way his face closed up immediately in denial. Horrified, Eve pulled her hand away. It wasn't possible still to be attracted to him! It had to be a sick joke! Getting her thoughts together was an incredible effort faced with that unwelcome reaction. To be attracted to someone who treated you with contempt was pure masochism. She felt panicky, but that fled after one more flickering glance at his face. He blamed her! The unfairness was a cold blast that settled her nerves instantly.

'You came alone, Mr Ramsay?' The level sound of her voice increased her confidence. 'I understood there would be more of you.'

There was ill-concealed rage behind those blue eyes. 'As we'll be working closely together, we'll dispense with the formalities, shall we?' he suggested brusquely, clearly finding the courtesy distasteful. 'You'd better call me Carl like everyone else. The others will be arriving presently. I came early in the hopes that Max would show me over the house.' He turned to the other man. 'You did say I could choose which rooms I wanted to use.'

Eve frowned, wondering if she was imagining the new undertones, and realised she wasn't when Max answered.

'I did, and the offer still stands. Surely you didn't expect me to withdraw it?' he challenged.

'I'm sure I don't know why it should occur to me,' Carl drawled with heavy irony that drew Max's laughter.

'I'm sure I don't know either—after all, I've nothing to hide. You may look wherever you wish, my dear Carl. Consider the house yours.'

Eve watched as the two men weighed each other up in silence, and finally it was Carl who inclined his head in wry acknowledgement.

'Eve would be delighted to show you round, wouldn't you, my dear?' Max smiled at her.

That wiped the smile from Carl's face, Eve noticed in grim amusement, though in reality she had no desire to accompany him either. 'I'm sure Carl would rather you did it, Max,' she interjected smoothly. 'You know so much more about the house than I do.'

Max looked regretful. 'Impossible, I'm afraid. I'm waiting for an important business call. You'll be happy with Eve, I'm sure, Carl.'

The battle lines drawn up, the two men disengaged. 'I'm sure I shall be, this time,' Carl observed sardonically, and turned to smile at her. 'Well, Eve, I'm all yours. You'd better lead the way.'

There was nothing to do but give in gracefully. She returned his smile with just as much sincerity and released Max's arm. 'We'll start downstairs then, shall we?'

'I'll arrange for coffee on the terrace when you come back,' Max called after them. 'Oh, and Eve, my dear...'

The tone was mild but, recognising it, she stiffened. 'Yes, Max?'

He smiled. 'Your hair.'

Automatically her hand went up to check. Damn, she had forgotten to pin it up. She had been busy since early morning with the last-minute arrangements, and then Carl's arrival had wiped it from her head. Max, being Max, had used the lapse to make a subtle statement of ownership. It wasn't lost on her companion, and Carl's cynical amusement set her teeth on edge.

Having made his point, Max departed, leaving them alone. Eve took a deep breath and dived in. With her hand she pointed out the way they were to go. The sooner this was over, the better.

'The house was built in the 1880s by the philanthropist——' she began in a monotone, and was interrupted before she could take another breath.

'You can spare me the history lesson. I've read all the books,' Carl remarked ungraciously as he fell into step beside her, hands in pockets.

Eve's teeth came together. 'Must you be so rude? This is hardly my idea of fun either!' she snapped.

'I don't need to ask what is,' he drawled cynically.

She came to an abrupt halt, swinging to face him with an acid smile. 'Considering our relative positions, don't you think it's a little unwise to insult me?' she pointed out.

To her surprise, Carl threw back his head and laughed. 'You really must be a dumb blonde. Max doesn't care if I insult you, sweetheart. I doubt if he'd even raise an eyebrow if I decided to jump you. He wants me here, you see. It's one big joke to him. However, I intend to see that he laughs on the other side of his face,' he finished, with a grim determination, thoughts far away.

Eve swallowed the humiliation of knowing he was right about her position and concentrated on the last part. He was being as mysterious as Max. 'Why does he want you here?'

Carl focused on her again. 'It's a delightful little nose, but I'd advise you to keep it out of other people's business. Anything I want Max to know, I'll tell him myself, without an intermediary. Is this corridor part of the tour?'

His sarcasm was hateful, assuming she was prying in order to tell tales. Yet, uncomfortably, she sensed that it might actually be what Max wanted, and she didn't like it. Without a word she continued on her way, every disc in her spine aware of him following her. Her thoughts were chaotic. There was more to this than just the film and she was the only one who didn't know what it was. She hated being used like this. Hated them both.

'What's wrong with your hair?' Carl's taunting query broke in on her.

She should have guessed he wouldn't leave that alone. Halting before a door, she summoned her composure, then looked round. 'I forgot to put it up this morning. Max doesn't care for loose hair,' she told him challengingly, knowing that her answer would call forth a scathing one of his own.

She wasn't disappointed. 'Is that so? Whatever Max wants, Max gets, right?' he mocked her with a curling lip.

If he thought to humble her, he had another think coming! One hand slid up to rest on her hip in a gesture that needed no subtitles. 'Why not? As I'm sure you're just waiting for the opportunity to point out, he is paying for it.' Violet eyes defied him even as she marvelled at herself. She was a better actress than she thought.

Carl simply came at her from another direction. 'And was he paying for that number you did on me? You didn't tell him about it, did you, Eve?'

Her brows rose. 'Aren't you rather forgetting your own part in it? It takes two to tango!' she retorted, wishing heartily that that ridiculous episode had never happened.

He smiled, teeth flashing whitely against his tan. 'My ego is fragile. That line generally works. I'm not used to failures.'

Inwardly she fumed. So she had been right, all he had wanted was a bedmate for the night, while she... Scrub that! He had been angry that night because she had frustrated him. He had thought he'd made it to home base! Thank God she had refused. It had been a very lucky escape. She had been a gullible, lonely, unhappy fool!

'If that's so, I'm surprised you didn't try harder, or do you always give up so easily? I'm amazed. A big, strong macho man like you!' she exclaimed mockingly.

He didn't like that. He didn't like it at all. About to make an angry retort, he stopped suddenly and looked thoughtful. He took one step nearer. 'Was I supposed to try harder, Eve?'

The dulcet question startled her into sudden wariness. 'What do you mean?'

'Did Max put you up to it?' he barked the query sharply, making her jump.

She didn't follow that at all. 'Why should he?' she returned in honest confusion.

The tension left him as quickly as it had come. 'Because, sweetheart, I know Max. It's entirely the sort of thing he would do. Like getting you into my film. He's killing two birds with one stone. Hindering me, and giving you what you want.'

That she felt compelled to argue with. 'Look, Mr Ramsay—— '

'Carl,' he interrupted smoothly.

'*Carl,*' she repeated heavily, 'I want you to know that this film business is all Max's idea.'

One of those damned eyebrows lifted. 'Really?' he drawled with heavy scepticism.

Her temper rose. 'Yes, really!' she snapped back. 'It's never been my intention to act, but Max wants me to, and...' She stopped at the look of derision on his face.

'Don't take me for a fool, Eve, because I didn't come down in the last shower. Max has already told me what this means to you, so let's cut out the protestations of innocence. Of which, by the way, we both know you don't possess a crumb. Let's get a few things straight. You may rule Max by crawling in and out of his bed, but to me you're nothing special. You're trying to make it the easy way, but I don't intend to smooth your path for you. I'll be running the show. There will be no running to Max when things don't go your way. By choice, I wouldn't let you within a hundred miles of this film, but I'm stuck with you. So I'll show you who's boss on this picture. You're going to work as you've never worked before, only this time on your feet, not on your back. Got it?'

Eve had never felt so utterly humiliated! What he was suggesting made her shrivel up inside, yet she would not let him see just how much that insulting tirade was hurting. She didn't even know why it should be when he was saying no more than everyone else thought. She hoped he put her pale face and tight lips down to anger. 'How could I fail to, when you have such a delightful way with words?'

He grinned, unrepentant. 'Stung, did it! Are you going to tell Max?' he taunted further.

She didn't bother to answer because they were both fully aware of the futility of such a move. She glared at him. 'I think I'm beginning to dislike you intensely, *Mr* Ramsay.'

He laughed drily. 'Only beginning? You're a lap behind me already!'

Eve's hand rested on the door-handle. At his reply, the door shot open with the force of her push as she strode angrily into the room. 'The morning-room,' she bit out raggedly, waving a hand haphazardly.

Carl followed her in more slowly, amusement at having scored off her curving his attractive mouth. Attractive? Oh, God! She mentally deleted the adjective and turned away, striving for a semblance of calm.

'We don't use this room very often. Max thought you and the others might care to use it for rehearsals and whatever.'

Carl glanced at her over his shoulder. 'You'll be part of the team too, or had you intended to cut yourself off from us whenever possible and join Max?'

She couldn't possibly tell him that she hadn't thought to be made welcome here once the others arrived. He would accuse her of playing for sympathy. 'Naturally, I'll do whatever you suggest, O master,' she declared with submissive sarcasm.

For once he seemed to see the funny side of it, and his grin was humorous. 'That will be the day!'

He really had a nice smile, she thought, watching him wandering around the room. It was a pity he didn't possess the personality to go with it.

'Yes, this should be fine.' His speculative gaze fell on her silent figure by the window. 'Tell me, Eve, have you ever done any acting?'

Apart from her Oscar-winning performances every day, did he mean? 'Only at school.'

Carl rested his hips against the sideboard and observed her critically. He looked as if she hadn't told him anything he didn't know, but the professional man was in control now. He had to calculate all the odds. 'Were you any good?'

Her lips twitched. 'We always closed to riotous applause, but you must allow for parental partisanship!' she joked naturally.

His brows went up, but he laughed, running a thoughtful hand around his neck. 'What did you play?'

The list actually ranged from Juliet and Cordelia to Lady Macbeth, with a side trip to Blanche in *A Streetcar Named Desire*. But she couldn't possibly tell him that. Her anger faded away. It made her uncomfortable, having to lie like this, and she raised a diffident shoulder. 'I played a fairy once, and a pixie,' she admitted, and heard him choke.

'Is that it? God! What the hell makes you think you can act?' he exploded, pacing to the window and glaring out.

Eve worried her lip. 'I was hoping you would tell me,' she offered uneasily.

'Did you ever have any lessons?'

'Sorry.'

'Any—arty film that shows you know how to follow direction?'

She straightened abruptly as shock took her breath away. 'How dare you?' she gasped furiously.

He faced her without amusement. 'You wouldn't be the first, darling,' he mocked her outrage.

She raked a trembling hand through her hair. 'God, your opinion of me is rock-bottom, isn't it?'

'Look on the bright side. It can't possibly get any lower, no matter what you do.'

Eve took a hasty step forward, hands clenched into fists. 'You're a despicable swine!'

Blue eyes glittered dangerously. 'And you——' He broke off, getting a hold of his temper with a visible effort as he walked back to the window. After a minute or two he sighed wearily. 'This isn't getting us anywhere. Perhaps we ought to continue with the tour now,' he suggested flatly.

Eve eyed that tense male back, and the anger drained away, leaving her limp. He was right. Exchanging insults was pointless. If they had to be caught in Max's trap together, the least they could do was be grown-up about it.

She led him over practically all the rest of the house in silence. He didn't ask to see the cellars or attics, but he insisted on looking into her bedroom and Max's. She witnessed the lift of his brows at the separate rooms, but he remained silent.

It wasn't until they approached the head of the stairs again that she broached a subject that was calculated to raise his temperature once more. However, she would rather reveal her ignorance to him alone than before a packed room.

Carl had stopped before one particular painting, a blue-eyed blonde with a sultry expression, who managed to make sitting in a chair remarkably sexy. Eve put the date about the mid-twenties by the flapper dress. It seemed an appropriate time to ask her question.

'What is the film about?'

He turned to her in absolute incredulity. 'Don't you know?'

She felt her colour rise. She should have asked Max, but, to be honest, it hadn't occurred to her. She couldn't have been sure anyway if he would tell her or prefer to keep her guessing. 'Max did say it was about previous owners of the house,' she returned defensively.

He shook his head. 'Haven't you even read the script? Max insisted on having a copy. I assumed, in your eagerness for stardom, you would at least have attempted to read the easy words.'

Her hand flew out and was caught in a crushing grip. Their eyes locked. 'That,' he said softly, 'would be a very bad mistake.'

Chest heaving, she glared at him, and couldn't repress a shiver. He caught it, and released her with a mocking smile before turning back to the portrait. Eve crossed her arms and rubbed her hands over them. Dear God, how could one man reduce her to such violence? She was appalled at her own behaviour and that made her hate him all the more.

When Carl started to speak, she had to pull herself together in order to hear it, for his voice was low, almost abstracted. He seemed almost obsessed by the woman, and her eyes were drawn to it too. It was almost obligatory to hold her breath. Who was she?

'In the twenties, during the early years of prohibition, there was a murder here. It led to one of the most controversial trials of the decade. Even now, no one can be sure that the right person was punished for the crime. Opinion is divided. The owner was a millionaire named Henry Maxwell. He lived here with his third wife, Velda, and two daughters from previous marriages, Ruth and Tania. One morning he was found dead at the bottom of the stairs. His skull had been crushed. There were three suspects: Velda, the eldest daughter, Ruth, and a greasy character called Jack Lloyd, the chauffeur. It was headline news, and so was the trial. That lasted months, and at the end it was Ruth who was found guilty and sentenced.'

It seemed almost indecent to interject a question, but she had to ask. 'You think the wrong one was convicted?'

Carl took a deep breath. 'If anyone was guilty, it was Velda. She walked away with the lion's share of Henry's money, and moved to Florida. With, of all people, Jack

Lloyd. A man who mysteriously disappears in a fishing accident, leaving her home and dry without any witnesses who might decide to turn nasty. Convenient, wouldn't you say?'

Eve looked from him to the portrait again. 'Who is she?'

He laughed grimly. 'That, darling, is Velda Maxwell herself.'

She gasped, although she felt she should have guessed, for somehow it didn't seem at all unlikely that the woman in the portrait should be involved in one, possibly two, murders. Those eyes were feral. She shivered.

'It's uncanny, I know, but ever since I've been here I've felt as if her eyes seem to follow me everywhere.' Once more she shivered, dismissing the uncomfortable fancy. 'But it should make a very good film. Murders always do. What made you choose this one?'

'It's always fascinated me. It's always cried out to be made into a film, but the climate wasn't right.'

Eve studied his thoughtful profile intently. 'You must be very grateful to Max for allowing you in here,' she declared softly, and was surprised to see his lips curl.

'Yes, very,' he drawled sardonically.

She waited for more, but the man beside her remained broodingly silent. She sighed. 'Which part am I playing?'

A deep blue gaze turned to mock her. 'Who do you think?' he drawled, and his eyes drew hers back to the portrait.

CHAPTER THREE

EVE descended the staircase in numb despair. Her loathing for Max grew. Doing a small part badly was one thing, but this! Of course he had known. Hadn't he said she looked the part? Velda Maxwell was the pivotal role, everything revolved around her. That meant the film's success rested on the actress playing her. Max's venomous nature had never been more obvious. He wanted to destroy more than just the film. He wanted Carl's credibility too.

The part she was expected to play in these machiavellian machinations made her feel as if she was going to be violently sick at any minute. What she couldn't understand was why Carl, who clearly felt strongly about the story, should let himself be manipulated by Max this way. It simply didn't make sense.

Mrs Addison, the housekeeper, met them in the hall. 'Mr Nilsson had to go out, miss. He sent his apologies and expects to be back for dinner. The other persons arrived some time ago, and they're taking coffee in the morning-room. Edward has taken their luggage to their rooms, as you requested. Will that be all?' Though there was nothing wrong with what she said, the way she said it was somehow less than polite.

Eve nodded coolly. She had tried in the beginning to strike a rapport with the woman, and been forced to give up. 'Yes, thank you, Mrs Danvers.' Appalled, she stopped, never imagining for an instant that her private thoughts as to who the woman reminded her of would spill out. Now she summoned up a smile in the face of icy displeasure. 'I'm so sorry, Mrs Addison, my mind was elsewhere. I'll ring if we require anything else.'

The housekeeper sniffed. 'Very good, miss,' she said, and went on her way.

Wilting, Eve wished she could have cut her tongue out. To say it at all was bad enough, but in Carl Ramsay's hearing was the outside of enough! Well, there was no time like the present to find out his reaction. She turned to eye him challengingly and found him laughing.

'Mrs Danvers?'

Eve smiled wryly. 'Well, she looks the type to push someone from a bedroom window.'

'She certainly doesn't like you. I wonder why that is,' he went on with a trace of mockery.

'You know that as well as I do,' she returned smoothly. 'She doesn't approve of me. I am, to coin an old-fashioned phrase, no better than I ought to be.' There was more than a tinge of bitterness hidden in the irony.

'And you think your position entitles you to more respect?' he queried. 'Has it occurred to you that you get so little respect because you set such little value on your own self-esteem? What self-respecting woman would choose to be kept solely for the pleasure of her body? It's degrading to your womanhood. Can't you see that, or has greed blinded you?'

That brief moment of empathy vanished, leaving her confusingly sad and angry. No, she wasn't blind, and he couldn't possibly know just how degraded she felt, how unclean. But they were things he had no right to challenge her with, right or wrong. 'Mr Ramsay, you can go to hell with my compliments. As for me, I'll go to hell by any means I choose. You aren't the guardian of my morals!' she bit out harshly.

'No, thank God. But your parents were. They don't appear to have done too good a job,' he sneered.

The mention of her parents was one goad too many. 'Leave my parents out of this!'

His smile was thin. 'Would they approve of what you're doing, Eve?'

She set her lips tight. 'I'm not going to discuss them with you.'

'So they wouldn't. Just what do they imagine their little ewe lamb is doing? Charity work?' The sarcasm was laid on with a trowel.

Eve produced a tight smile. 'Oh, very amusing, Carl, I must remember that one.'

He regarded her curiously. 'Doesn't anything I say make you feel ashamed?'

Violet eyes widened. 'Is *that* what you're trying to do?' she said with a chuckle, while inside her stomach churned at the hypocrisy of defending like crazy a position that revolted her. 'Oh, come now, surely you're not so naïve to believe I could feel shame?' she chided, and faltered, because for one crazy instant she thought she saw disappointment reflected in those deep blue eyes. Then she decided she was the naïve one for being absurdly dejected to realise it was just a trick of the light.

'Had I been, meeting you would certainly have been an education,' he told her coldly. 'We'd better join the others before they think they've been abandoned.'

Eve was only too happy to go, and withdraw from a conversation that had made her feel increasingly ill at ease. The door of the morning-room had been left ajar, and as they approached it voices could be heard quite distinctly.

'Anyway,' a young female voice was saying, 'I think it's kind of her father to let us use the actual house.'

There followed a collective groan, then one drawling, masculine voice continued. 'Jenny, sweet thing, where have you been all your life? I said he was her sugar-daddy, not her father. In return for a bit of hanky-panky, this dumb blonde gets to screw up our film!'

The words brought Eve to a halt outside the door, heat scorching her cheeks. Behind her, Carl reached past to push the door wide, and at the same time his low voice mocked her. 'What did you expect? That they'd welcome you with open arms? Dick's wife was down for the part you now have. I wouldn't look for an ally in that quarter.'

A cool silence had fallen on the room as he urged her inside ahead of him. Looking at each of the four faces before her, Eve knew that she would find no friend here. They all resented her presence, and how could she possibly blame them for it? It wasn't going to get any better either, so what she must do was remember why she was doing it, and square her shoulders for what must follow.

She watched silently as Carl went forward to greet his stars, and it was clear they were all old friends. A curious little ache started up inside her as she watched the genuine pleasure light up his face, transforming it, and his laughter was as rich as she first remembered it. She realised she was only feeling sorry for herself, otherwise she wouldn't be wishing he would be that way with her. Maybe the others were deceived by his *bonhomie*, but she had to remember that she knew differently. There was more than a little of the opportunist cad about Carl Ramsay.

He was back to the man she was familiar with when he turned to introduce her to each one in turn. Nina Marshall, a striking brunette of about Eve's age, was to play Ruth Maxwell, the older daughter. Jenny Ivers, who was to play Tania, was still only a teenager herself. Rolf Anderson, Ruth's fiancé, was being played by one of the famous brat pack, Miles Warrender. Lastly there was Dick Favell, whose wife had been going to take the part Eve now had. Looking like Burt Reynolds' younger brother, he was taking the part of the chauffeur, Jack Lloyd.

The look he gave her was acid, and he was clearly looking for a fight when he said brusquely, 'Just what acting experience have you had, Miss Hunter?'

Carl then surprised Eve completely by not adding the mocking rider she expected, but saying with considerable authority, 'Eve admits to not being an actress, Dick, so I'm relying on all of you to give her all the help and encouragement you can. She may just surprise us, I hope.'

Dick Favell snorted in disgust. 'Oh, come on, Carl! You know we don't have a hope of making a film worth a damn!'

Carl rested his weight on a corner of the table and crossed his arms, eyes roving each of them in turn. 'I take it that's how you all feel?' He received four nods. 'Then it's time for some plain speaking. I'm not exactly overjoyed by the arrangement myself. However, the bottom line is this—there would be no film without this house, and no house without Eve.'

'Hell, there are other houses!' Dick snarled. 'What's so special about this one that anyone will notice?'

Eve very much wanted to know the answer to that, too. Carl seemed to be looking at Nina, and when Eve tipped her head to see she saw the brunette smile encouragingly. So, she thought, Nina knows something too! Her curiosity was piqued.

Carl smiled, but it was full of grim determination, not humour. 'This house is special all right, Dick. It's the only place that will add something unique to the film.'

Jenny giggled. 'You're making it sound very mysterious,' she said with an expressive shiver. 'What sort of something?'

Carl grinned back at her. 'If I told you, I'd lose the element of surprise.' He came to his feet abruptly and clapped his hands. 'Right, if no one else has any objections, let's get down to business. We're on a tight schedule, and I intend to have no more delays than necessary. Max has been generous enough to give us the run of the house, but not without a time-limit. So, get your scripts, sit down, and let's get started.'

Eve found herself seated between Nina and Jenny. The younger girl gave her a cheeky smile. 'It makes you feel like royalty living here, doesn't it?' she declared confidentially, then blushed a fiery red when she realised who she was talking to.

Eve half smiled, feeling sorry for the girl whose nature was to be open and trusting, and who must be finding this situation uncomfortable. 'Sometimes,' she agreed, to put her at her ease.

'Now,' Carl began, opening a briefcase that must have been brought from his car. From it he drew two folders and pushed one across the table to Eve. 'I suggest that to begin with we read through the script without any attempt at characterisation, just to give Eve an idea of the plot. After that we'll go over one or two scenes in detail so that I can get some idea of what she can do.'

So they began. Eve was nervously aware that she was the focus of everyone's attention, so much so that the first half of the script barely registered, they were just words that she forced out from a dry mouth. The latter half, including the trial scenes, came across very impressively though. It made her turn back to the beginning to discover just who had written it. Carl's name fairly leapt out at her, and she looked at him with a new and grudging respect.

This whole project really was important to him. He had written the script he was about to direct. He had insisted on using the real location, despite having to be dictated to by Max. That spoke of something more than just a whim. But what? A mission? Hadn't Max called it precisely that?

'Eve.' She jumped guiltily at the sharp sound of her name and turned to Carl. He was briskly leafing through the pages. 'Start from page thirty-six. Give the scene a little more depth. It will help you feel the character of Velda.'

She must have read it before, but she didn't recall it. By the fourth line her stomach was churning and the nails of her left hand were biting deeply into her palm to stop her from showing any sign of her feelings. Oh, yes, it certainly gave her a very clear insight into Velda, and Carl had chosen the scene deliberately. The wife was doing everything she could to seduce her stepdaughter's fiancé! It showed her up to be an amoral, self-seeking bitch. Out of all the scenes Carl could have chosen, he had picked that one to underline just what his own opinion of Eve was.

She felt sick, but she kept on reading in a carefully blank voice. Inside, her heart seethed with a black anger. He was the lowest, most contemptible creature on earth. Only minutes ago she had been toying, actually toying, with the idea of not being quite as bad an actress as she could be, but not any more. Now she would see him in hell first.

Eve reached the end of the scene and looked up. Across the table, violet eyes almost black with fury met mocking blue ones. They reminded her that he had said he wasn't going to make it easy for her.

'Do you get the feel of her?' he asked mildly.

The others seated around the table would have to have been totally insensitive not to have picked up the vibrations bouncing off the two of them. They awaited her answer in a bated hush, Dick with avid interest, but Nina frowning darkly.

Eve was so intensely angry that she shook with it, yet her voice issued forth, laden with husky amusement. 'Oh, yes, I believe I do. Let me say it for you, Carl. It's a perfect piece of type-casting.'

Jenny gasped, Dick burst out laughing. Even Miles smiled, but Nina's frown didn't lift at all.

Carl's eyes gleamed. 'Good, that's what I thought. Now we'll start again from the top, and this time we'll put some emotion into it.'

So they did the scene again. Eve tried. She made sure they all realised she was trying, but somehow the scene became dull and lifeless. It was a masterpiece of acting she was proud of. It was hard to look up in the fraught silence at the end and not burst out laughing. The expression on Carl's face was balm to her bruised spirit.

Across the table, Carl's breath hissed in angrily. 'By comparison, a dead fish would be positively eloquent,' he drawled derisively, clearly holding on to his temper by a thread. 'This woman married a man forty years her senior, solely for his money. Their sex-life has been virtually non-existent. She's frustrated. Her wandering eye has lit on Rolf and she wants him. Nothing is going to get in her way as she goes after what she wants. This is seduction, not afternoon tea with a maiden aunt!'

Eve lowered her lids to hide her gleam of triumph. 'I'm trying,' she insisted.

The derision expanded. 'What you are trying, Eve, is my patience—a not inexhaustible commodity right now. So why don't you take advantage of personal experience, imagine life with Max, and then give me some damned emotion?'

Her gasping intake of breath echoed Nina's 'Carl!' Eve went white with fury. With jerky movements she flipped back pages.

'If you want emotion, *Mr* Ramsay,' she spat thickly, pain expanding in an excruciating wave, 'you can damn well have it!' So saying, she launched into an impassioned rendering that brought the character to angry life. After a stunned moment, the others quickly stepped into their own roles or sat back and listened in silence.

For the third time they faced each other. Eve, chest heaving, Carl in an ice-cold rage that dripped from every cutting word. 'That certainly had the felicity of passion, however inapposite. Perhaps I should insist that Max joins in every rehearsal; he certainly seems to…inspire…you!' he finished insultingly, and, thrusting back his chair, he rose to his feet and left through the french doors. They had a perfect view of his stiff-backed figure striding out angrily across the lawn.

Eve shuddered and closed her eyes. Damn him! She heard chairs scrape back as the others tactfully decided to leave.

'Well, that was novel,' Dick declared drily on his way out. 'I've never been to a preliminary reading quite like it before. This film might turn out to be interesting, after all!' The door clicked shut.

A gentle but firm hand on her wrist made Eve jump. She opened her eyes to see Nina uncurling her own fingers from her palm and pressing a clean white handkerchief to the bloody nail marks. The sight shocked her, for she hadn't even felt herself doing it.

'If I were you, I'd put some antiseptic on those,' the brunette advised sensibly.

Eve met the thoughtful brown eyes warily. 'Thanks, I will.'

'I'm sorry you had to run into Carl's temper. He's under a lot of pressure right now,' Nina apologised.

'Really?' Weren't they all!

Those brown eyes remained uncomfortably steady and thoughtful. 'Actually, I've never seen him behave quite that rudely before. Do you mind if I ask you a question? Has something happened between you and Carl?'

Eve dropped her eyes, her whole body tensing. 'Yes. We met, and instantly fell in hate with each other. Don't tell me you hadn't noticed!' she retorted sarcastically, then instantly regretted her nastiness. She shouldn't be taking it out on Nina. 'I'm sorry, that was rude. It must be catching.' It was a feeble joke, but Nina smiled.

'If he was rough on you, don't take it too personally. As I say, he's got a lot on his mind. He'll probably apologise later.'

Eve had to agree, because there was no point in revealing that it was a personal thing. Life was complicated enough as it was. One thing she did know—Max might be benefiting from her actions, but from now on ensuring the film flopped would give her the greatest satisfaction.

Feeling her spirits lift with this new determination, she pushed herself to her feet. 'I was going to freshen up before lunch. I'll show you up to your room at the same time, if you like,' she offered, and Nina took her up on it with a smile.

Lunch wasn't a particularly comfortable meal. Carl returned in a brooding mood that threw a pall over the table. The afternoon was spent, under Carl's irascible direction, going over various scenes that were to be shot in the house, and by the end of it everyone's nerves were in tatters. Eve had read her lines with the same earnest lifelessness, but Carl hadn't attempted to use his previous tactics. His thoughts, when he closed his copy of the script, were hidden from everyone.

He sat back in his chair and observed them all slowly. 'OK, here's the plan so far. The crew will be arriving tomorrow, and they'll need a few days to set everything up. By then I should have decided which rooms we're going to use for which scenes. I'll get the yellow sheets to you as soon as possible, so, unless you're wanted in wardrobe, you might as well take advantage of the brief holiday and see some of the sights.'

'Gee, I always wanted to see the sights of...where exactly are we anyway?' Miles put in as he began the general exodus.

'Not you, Eve.' Carl's voice halted her move to leave too. 'Shut the door, would you?' he added quietly as he left the chair to go to the window, standing there with his back to her and hands in his trouser pockets. She did as he asked, then waited stiffly for him to speak. 'Did you expect me to apologise for this morning?' he asked shortly, not turning round.

'No.' Her reply was just as curt.

Carl flexed tired shoulders. 'All the same, I do. I usually manage to keep my personal feelings out of my work. In future I'll do my best to follow that principle.'

And that was an apology? 'So what you're saying is, you're not apologising for your opinions, just for airing them in public?' she clarified, seething again. 'Forgive me if I feel somewhat underwhelmed by your generosity. If that is all, I think I'll go and recover from the shock.'

He swung round angrily. 'No, it is not all. Let's get something straight right now. I will not put up with your tantrums either here or on the set. We are here to work, and that is what we are going to do. The others may have a holiday, but you don't. Now I suggest you take that script away with you and study it, very carefully, page by page. By the time we get around to rehearsals, I'll expect you to have at least a good working knowledge of it. Understood?' The look in his eyes came straight from the arctic wastes.

'Perfectly.'

'Then you may go,' he dismissed her, and turned back to the window.

Eve collected the script and left. She would have loved to slam the door on the supercilious beast, but she had discovered that for some reason it was physically impossible to do that in this house. Instead, frustrations had to be left to ferment inside her. One day, she promised herself, she would make him sorry.

Max came into her room as she was fastening diamond drops in her ears. Dinner was always formal, but tonight he had insisted they dress up to celebrate the start of the film. So she was wearing royal-blue satin, with a straight skirt and a boned bodice that plunged dramatically. Her make-up was perfectly applied and her hair folded into a smart French pleat. The combination was at once haughty and seductive.

Eve watched Max's soft-footed approach in the mirror, her heart picking up speed as it always did when he was around. She never quite knew which way he was going to jump. He must have been home some time, for he was already dressed for dinner. Coming up behind her, he rested proprietorial hands on her shoulders and watched their twin reflections. His eyes gleamed as they followed the *décolletage* of her dress.

'I hear filming should start in a day or two. Are you excited, my dear?'

Eve reached out a hand for the necklace that matched the earrings. 'No,' she said flatly.

Max laughed and relieved her of the delicate chain, fastening it about her neck himself and allowing his fingers to trail down her spine until she shivered. 'You rehearsed, too. How did that go?'

'Badly,' she admitted, and surreptitiously watched for his reaction.

'And how did Carl take it?'

Eve knew by his very blandness that the answer was important. 'As you would expect. He was angry,' she told him, wondering why it should be that, however much she detested Carl Ramsay, as soon as Max became so quietly malevolent her determination weakened.

Grey eyes were dancing at some private joke. 'Perfect. I trust you'll see it stays that way. Now, we mustn't keep our guests waiting any longer. My dear——' He offered her his arm and she took it, allowing him to escort her from the room. As they slowly descended the staircase, though, it appeared he hadn't finished. 'I've been thinking, my dear Eve, how much more helpful it would be if you accompanied Carl on his tours of the house, as my amanuensis. But for pressure of work, I would do it myself. I find the whole idea fascinating, and I would be interested to know just how he intends to go about it.'

Eve's brow creased. 'Go about what?'

'Why, searching for the right location for the filming, of course,' he said blandly, and then chuckled at his own joke, leaving Eve bewildered. 'I've made a study of the subject myself over the years, though not, I'm sure, as detailed as Ramsay's. You'll have gathered he believes Ruth Maxwell was innocent. I'd be fascinated to know why, and how he intends to prove it, but you know how cagey these fellows are. He won't say a word. Perhaps you, my dear Eve, will succeed where I have failed.'

It all sounded very plausible, but somehow Eve knew that along the line the explanation had changed. 'I'll do what I can,' she responded dutifully.

'I know you will, but there is one thing that will have to change. I've noticed a certain . . . chilliness in your attitude to our Mr Ramsay. That must go. You'll learn nothing by being so cold. Be friendly, my dear. Get close to the man. Get me the results I want, my dear Eve, and I may just give you that present you long for,' he finished, holding the agreement over her head like a carrot for the donkey.

There was no need for her to answer, for what could she say, except agree, and he knew that already. She shuddered at the thought of getting 'close' to Carl Ramsay. She was already closer than she wanted to be.

Dinner was a sparkling success. Max was a charming host. Eve watched from her seat at one end of the table as he dazzled his guests with his wit and charm. She could see him feeding the egos of the two young men, and treating Jenny as if he were an indulgent grandfather. He very soon had them eating out of his hand. Only Carl and Nina remained untouched. The brunette, for whatever reasons of her own, responded with a polite reserve, while Carl sat back in his chair and watched the by-play from behind impregnable blue eyes.

Catching Max's eye, Eve realised that she had failed so far to hold up her own role as hostess, that it was her duty to keep Carl entertained. Reluctantly she addressed him now.

'Have you made many films, Carl?' she asked coolly, and drew those incredible eyes to hers.

'Quite a few,' he responded sardonically.

She told herself to keep calm in the face of his unhelpfulness. 'Were they murder stories too?'

'Some,' he said with a grin.

Her eyes flashed. 'You're being deliberately difficult!' she muttered fiercely.

'Tsk, tsk, what *would* Emily Post say?' he reproved softly.

Eve set her lips. 'I'm trying to be polite. You could at least help.'

His grin was unrepentant. 'Sorry. So tell me, how many jigsaw puzzles do you get through in a week?' he went on blandly.

Eve blinked. 'Jigsaw puzzles?'

'Yes, you know—the odd-shaped little bits of wood that fit together to make a picture,' he enlarged helpfully.

She drew in her breath. 'I do know what a jigsaw is, thank you!' she snapped back.

'So did Marion Davies. Legend, according to Welles, has it that she got through a fair number while awaiting her lover's pleasure,' Carl elucidated finally.

Eve's fingers clenched on her napkin. 'I see, we're back to that again, are we?' she said tightly, smiling for Max's benefit.

Carl shrugged. 'It seemed...appropriate. More wine?' he held up the bottle and she pushed her glass towards him.

'I'm trying to like you, Mr Ramsay, but you're making it very hard,' she declared frigidly.

He looked at her in mock surprise. 'Are you? Why bother?'

Eve gave up, snapping her teeth together. 'Why indeed?' Pushing back her chair, she prepared to bring the meal to an end, only Carl's hand coming down on hers stopped her. Her eyes shot to his and found them alive with laughter.

'Better luck next time,' he said softly, and let her go.

There would be no next time, she thought wildly, as she left with Jenny and Nina, leaving the men to their port and cigars. But she had barely gone beyond the door before realising that of course there would be, for she had Max to consider. She was beginning to feel as if she was in a living nightmare.

Over coffee, Jenny rhapsodised over the magnificence of the location she found herself in, and her host. Eve listened in mounting dismay as the girl revealed how enchanted by it all she was, and realised there was a very real danger that she saw Max as some sort of prince instead of the devil he was. She hoped she was imagining it, but she promised to keep an eye on the girl, and if it looked as if Max was about to make a conquest she would take steps to stop it. She would not stand idly by and see such a sweet innocent destroyed, whatever the consequences to herself.

When the men rejoined them, Max took up a position on the arm of Eve's chair, one arm resting lightly across her shoulders. His hand, with the large ruby ring on his finger, smoothed over her skin rhythmically as he talked. Eve forced herself to relax and allow him the freedom. She tried not to look at Carl, but she could feel the force of his gaze on her, tugging her like a magnet until she had to lift her eyes. He made no effort to hide his contempt and a little colour stole into her cheeks.

'Eve tells me she wasn't much help to you today,' Max declared ruefully.

'You can say that again!' Dick snorted immediately.

Max's eyes narrowed on him for a moment, and then passed on to Carl. 'I know she doesn't have the experience, but I'm sure she'll put her heart and soul into the part. It means a lot to her.'

Carl's blue eyes dropped to Eve's violet ones. 'If it does, perhaps you can persuade her to repeat her best performance. At one point this morning she was very nearly brilliant,' he drawled smoothly.

Eve went into shock. She knew precisely what that dig at her was meant to convey, but to Max it would seem to have an entirely different connotation. Her heart flew into her throat and beat there sickeningly fast. A cold chill ran down her spine as fingers closed on her shoulder.

'Was she now?' Max declared in delight, and tipped her head up to smile down at her. 'Then I must definitely have a word with her. With things going so well, I wouldn't want anything to go wrong at this stage,' he finished softly, letting her go again.

The hours that followed were a nightmare. Eve went on as if nothing had happened, all the time knowing that as soon as they were alone Max would demand an explanation. Which he did the minute the others followed Carl's lead and went up to their rooms. Not that he said a word as they faced each other, standing by the door he had closed to block off her retreat. It was the long, chilly silence of his regard that forced her into speech.

'I'm afraid this morning was my fault. If I produced the effect Carl wanted, it was by accident. He made me **angry**, you see. It was an accident and it won't happen again,' she promised flatly.

'For your sake, I hope it won't,' he replied, and like a darting snake his hand shot out and dealt her a stinging slap on her cheek. 'That will serve as a reminder for you. Now you may go to bed, my dear.'

Tight-lipped and inwardly shaking, she let herself out and shut the door behind her. Sagging back on it, she raised a hand to her stinging cheek, and angry tears flooded her eyes. It was all Carl's fault. He despised her so much, he couldn't resist taunting her. He had given her just one more reason to get her revenge.

The sound of footsteps caused her to glance to her left, and her eyes widened as she saw Carl coming towards her from the morning-room. He wouldn't need to be a genius to guess what had happened, and the idea of his knowing it made her cringe. Dropping her hand, she picked up her skirts and ran. She had no idea that Carl had followed her up the stairs until his hand stopped her from shutting her bedroom door.

It was an unequal fight, for he was far stronger, and he pushed his way inside easily. Eve turned her back on him, but he swung her round, and she was forced to stand there, rigid with humiliation, as he tipped her face to the light with amazingly gentle fingers. She had to swallow hard because suddenly she wanted to cry. She wanted to drop her head against the broad shoulder before her, and cry her heart out. And that was crazy, because they loathed each other.

Carl let her go and disappeared into her bathroom. She really should have moved then. Made some sort of effort to gain control of the situation, but she didn't seem to have the energy. She heard him moving about, and then he was back, pressing a cold flannel to her cheek.

'How often does this happen?' he asked grimly.

'It's never happened before. Max isn't usually a violent man,' she said unsteadily, wishing she could stop shaking. Somehow Carl wasn't making it any easier.

His eyes shifted to hers, holding them. 'What did you do? Say something he didn't like?'

There was anger in those midnight-blue depths, but directed against who or what she had no idea. 'Why should you care?' she retorted dully, finding the strength to pull away from him at last.

Carl looked grim. 'Because no man has the right to knock a woman about, and no woman should be expected to put up with it,' he declared curtly.

He clearly held strong views on the subject, and it made her uncomfortable about her ungraciousness, enough to say stupidly, 'Even women in my position?'

It made him frown angrily. 'No man worthy of calling himself that should hit a woman, whatever her position. Nor does he merit protecting. If this is a habit, don't condone it by playing dumb. Tell me and I'll do something about it.'

Eve felt like squirming at her own behaviour, especially in view of his offer. As a consequence, her reply was brittle. 'Thanks, but there won't be any need. As I told you, this has never happened before.'

'And you'd better make sure it doesn't happen again,' he growled just as tautly. 'If he's knocking you around, make-up may have a hard job covering the evidence. That could hold up the shooting.'

Eve gasped. And she had just been starting to believe he actually cared! She should have known where his priorities lay. Her anger boiled over once more. 'That wouldn't do, would it? Relax, Carl, this is a one-off. I may have stepped out of line, but I'm a quick learner. Your precious film is safe. Now, I'd be grateful if you'd just go.'

He visibly bit back an angry retort, lips thinning as his eyes went to the connecting door. 'Expecting Max?' he drawled insolently.

Her chin shot up. 'And if I am, precisely what business is it of yours?' she challenged, eyes flashing angry sparks.

Carl's jaw tautened, a muscle jumping there. 'For a minute I thought perhaps you needed help, but I was wrong. I apologise for intruding where my gallantry wasn't needed. I'll know better next time. Goodnight, Eve. Pleasant dreams.' Even the door seemed to close sarcastically behind him.

She stood there shaking with rage that couldn't be expressed. 'I hate you, Carl Ramsay! I hate you, do you hear me?' she cried in a sibilant whisper, crushing the flannel between white-knuckled fists. Then in a helpless gesture she flung it at the place where he had been.

Sinking on to the bed, she rested her head in her hands. How could she ever do what Max wanted and get close to that hateful man? He would never believe her change of mind. Yet she had to try, and make it convincing.

She was so close to getting her freedom! Of course, Max could be tricking her again, but she had to believe him. So there had to be a way, there just had to be.

CHAPTER FOUR

Eve stared at Carl's back and chewed her lip irresolutely. There was only one plan she had been able to come up with during a virtually sleepless night, and she was about to put it into effect. She didn't know why she felt so nervous. Unless it was because she didn't want to do it. Yet she had been doing things she didn't want to on Max's orders for months without getting jittery. She just pulled down the shutters and did it. Somehow, though, the shutters just didn't seem to work around Carl. She hated him for making her so vulnerable again.

But all this wasn't getting her anywhere. Taking a ragged breath, she walked into the room where Carl had just finished a highly involved discussion with his technicians. He had risen early and gone out long before she'd left her room, so she had not seen him since last night, nor had a chance to gauge his mood. She hoped for the best, but braced herself for the worst. He heard her footsteps and turned, watching broodingly as she picked her way through a mass of cables.

This morning he was dressed for work in faded jeans and T-shirt. It made him look approachable, not to mention vitally attractive. Eve was aware that her blue silk dress was totally incongruous in these surroundings. It added to her unease just when she needed to be at her most cool. She came to a halt a foot away.

'I've been looking for you,' she began unevenly, and tensed when his mobile eyebrows rose.

'Why the sudden desire for my company?' he quizzed coldly, raking eyes catching the small betraying signs of her tension.

It wasn't a very auspicious beginning. Not that that surprised her. She licked dry lips. 'Could we talk?'

'I thought we were.'

Eve caught her breath and ordered herself not to get angry. 'I mean, somewhere a little more private than this,' she explained levelly.

Carl regarded her through narrowed eyes before shrugging. 'Let's go on the terrace if it's that important. You've got five minutes.'

She gritted her teeth, holding back an angry retort, and preceded him out into the sunshine. There was a stone seat further along and she made for it, sitting down and holding on to its coolness. Carl propped himself against the low wall opposite, crossing arms and ankles.

'OK, what is it?' he asked impatiently.

Eve's fingers tightened on the stone, the only sign of her reaction to his abruptness. 'I want to apologise for last night,' she began, not quite able to meet his eyes as she forced the words out. 'I realise you were only trying to be...kind. I shouldn't have been angry with you. I was upset, you see. I'm sorry if I was rude,' she apologised and waited.

Carl let out his breath in an explosive sigh. 'And that's what you brought me out here to hear?' he declared incredulously. 'OK, fair enough, apology accepted. Now, if you'll excuse me...' He made to leave, and Eve shot quickly to her feet.

'No. Wait, Carl, please, I... There's something else.' God, how she hated to plead, especially with this man! Damn you, Max!

Carl frowned at the agitated movements of her hands, and the tell-tale pulse beating in her throat. He resumed his seat, curiosity aroused. 'I'm listening.'

This was the crunch point. Everything rested on her ability to convince him. Unable to meet those penetrating eyes, Eve rubbed her palms together nervously and went to lean on the wall some feet away where she didn't have to look at him while she spoke.

'We...we got off to a bad start the other day, didn't we? I don't want to go into who was to blame or anything like that. But this...situation...is going to be hard enough without us being at each other's throat all the time. We've got to work together for some weeks, and this atmosphere won't help. I thought that the very least we should do, as adults, is try to get along.'

She swallowed and looked at him sideways, trying to gauge his reaction, but Carl was staring down at his feet.

'Well?' she prompted. 'What do you think?'

He looked up suddenly, expression inscrutable. 'It's a valid point. As you say, we're not children. Could you do it?' he asked sceptically.

Relief at getting over the hurdle, or very nearly, brought a smile to her lips. 'I'd be willing to give it a try. How about you?'

There was a light in Carl's eyes that she couldn't interpret, and then he smiled too. 'OK, we'll give it a go. For the sake of the film,' he added drily.

Eve gave a breathy laugh. 'Yes, of course, for the film.'

They stood there facing each other and the gleam in Carl's eyes deepened. 'Well, now, having achieved this new spirit of co-operation, we shouldn't let such a golden opportunity go by, should we?' he declared smoothly.

Uncertain of his meaning, Eve's smile was doubtful. 'No. No, of course not.'

'Now why is it you look as if you've caught a tiger by the tail, and rather wished you hadn't?' he mused ironically.

Eve felt the heat invade her cheeks at the accuracy of his words. An acid reply was on the tip of her tongue when he laughed.

'Don't spoil it. We've been doing quite well so far, and you may find out that I'm not such a bad fellow after all. All I was about to suggest was that you join me this morning and find out what goes on behind the scenes. You might even find it interesting.'

Eve was caught. How could she refuse if she had meant what she'd said? She prayed her forbearance would last the experience. 'All right,' she nodded, and tried to look enthusiastic.

Carl grinned and shook his head, but said nothing, merely inviting her to follow him. Eve took a deep breath and closed her eyes for an instant. So far, so good, she thought, and went after him. She found herself far more interested than she had expected. That, she realised, was due entirely to Carl. He loved everything about his chosen profession, and it came over as he talked. She listened with interest to his discussions with the various technicians, and began to appreciate the varied knowledge a director had to have in order to do his job properly. Add to that the vision necessary to see the parts as a whole and get that on film, and it made up a very talented man. Despite herself, Eve was impressed. Time fairly flew by, and all her earlier misgivings fell by the wayside. By the time everything stopped at lunchtime she was willing to admit that he wasn't all bad after all.

Looking around her, Eve discovered that order had very nearly been achieved from chaos, and shook her head. 'It's incredible. How do you do it?'

Carl looked about him in approval. 'Practice, and a good strong whip,' he drawled drily, and turned, arrested, at the sound of her laughter. He set his jaw tight and a nerve ticked for a second before he relaxed again, his face smoothing out blandly. 'So, we've survived the morning. What do you propose for this afternoon?'

Eve, sobered by the rapid change of expressions on his face, collected herself together in a hurry. 'Do you think we ought to push our luck?'

'Are you saying you've had enough?' he neatly put the onus back on her.

'No, but I did think that you might have.'

Blue eyes mocked her. 'When I have, be sure I'll let you know.'

And that she could well believe, but inside she had a warm glow at the realisation that he must have enjoyed the morning too. Perhaps they really were going to reach a new understanding. 'In that case, I could show you over the house again. You didn't have much time yesterday,' she suggested.

Carl rubbed a thoughtful hand over his chin, 'Sounds like a good idea to me. I've got to choose the rooms anyway. OK, you can bring a pad and pencil too. You may as well make yourself useful taking notes.'

Eve relaxed a little more. If Carl was going to continue in this mood, it wasn't going to be bad at all. 'You're the boss,' she acknowledged wryly.

Blue eyes gleamed for an instant, then faded. 'I'm having lunch with my assistant, so I'll meet you back in the hall at about two o'clock. Agreed?'

'All right. Two o'clock, pad in hand,' she nodded assent.

Carl turned to leave, but after a few steps he hesitated and turned back. 'You don't think Max will object to my monopolising your time?' he asked as an afterthought.

The question jolted Eve's nerves, and for a second her vocal chords were strangulated in her throat. Finally, she managed to emit a wobbly, 'No.'

He nodded, apparently satisfied, and went away whistling. Eve knew a moment of doubt. Was it all too easy? Did he know what she was doing? She couldn't see how. Besides, she berated herself, there wasn't time for doubts. Max wanted results, and she had to furnish them. She couldn't afford to look any gift-horse in the mouth.

They met in the hall at two. Eve had taken the opportunity to change into cotton trousers and a lemon blouse. In one hand she carried a notepad, in the other a large roll of paper. Carl looked at it with some interest as he came in through the front door.

'What's that?' he asked when he reached her.

Eve handed it over. 'Max thought you might like to have them. They're the plans of the house.' She watched him curiously as he unrolled it, for the self-same amusement she had seen on Max's face when he'd given it to her at lunch was reflected now on Carl's.

He only gave it one brief look before rolling it up again. 'Thoughtful of him, but I have my own copy.'

Eve blinked. 'You do?' she exclaimed in surprise, wondering why on earth he should have plans of Max's house. 'Is that usual?'

'Perhaps not. In this case, though, the plans were used in evidence at the trial, to show where the body was found in relation to the suspects' alleged whereabouts. It came as part of my research material.'

That made sense. 'Oh, I see. I expect Max didn't realise.'

Carl gave her an old-fashioned look as he tapped the roll thoughtfully. 'Just the same, I'll keep this, for the sake of comparison. Never know what you might find. A discrepency here, an anomaly there.' He focused on her puzzled face and smiled blandly. 'Ready? Then we'll start at the top this time.'

They did. Right at the top, in the attics. There was electric light, so they didn't have any trouble seeing their way. These days the rooms were only used for storage, but once upon a time they had served as the servants' quarters. Eve shuddered at the idea, and doubted that any self-respecting employee would put up with being stuck under the eaves, at the mercy of all weathers, in the nineties.

Nothing, it appeared, had ever been thrown away. The rooms were a positive treasure-trove. There was furniture unlimited, either broken or simply out of fashion. Chests of clothes and books. Sporting equipment, even an upright piano in one corner. Eve was enthralled, and could happily have sat down and waded through it all for hours. She was also more than a little mystified.

'I don't remember any scenes set up here in the script,' she called out, brushing dust from the surface of a roll-top desk.

'I'm glad to hear you've been doing your homework. There aren't,' Carl answered from behind a wardrobe, 'but I didn't see that as any reason for not looking. You never know what you'll find.'

Eve held her breath. 'Are you looking for anything in particular?' she asked as nonchalantly as she could. If he was, then Max would be interested.

'No,' came the distant and amused reply.

Pulling a face, Eve eased her way towards the back. 'There are some pictures against the wall. Who would want to tuck them away up here?' she wondered, frowning, and shifted part of a brass bedstead.

'Where?' Carl materialised at her side. 'Hmm, let me see.'

They were placed face to face, and he turned them both towards the light. Dusty, but otherwise undamaged, the larger was of a thickset man, with greying hair and a dour face. He was standing, with one hand rested on the back of an ornate chair, the other, with a large jewelled ring on one finger, tucked into the fob pocket of his waistcoat. The other portrait was the head and shoulders of a young woman who bore a striking resemblance to the man. Yet there was a sweetness of expression, a love of life and a sparkling sense of humour in the brown eyes that was lacking in the man. She was more used to smiling.

'The mystery is explained,' Carl stated evenly, eyes on the woman, brushing away dust with a handkerchief. 'Meet Henry Maxwell and his daughter Ruth.'

With a faint gasp, and regardless of the dust, Eve sank to her knees, studying them both closely. There was a warmth in the young woman's eyes and a sweet curve to her lip. 'I don't believe it. That face couldn't kill anybody, let alone her father,' she denied firmly.

'Twelve good men and true didn't agree with you,' Carl returned pointedly, his eyes never leaving her face, a faint smile hovering about his lips.

'You don't think she did it either,' Eve reminded him.

Carl stacked the pictures back carefully and stood up. 'Not because of the way she looked.'

Eve rose too and dusted herself off. Her heart was thudding erratically. Here was a golden opportunity to get the information Max wanted, and she hadn't had to do a thing. Carl was about to reveal it all—if she was careful enough.

'Then you have another reason for thinking it?' she prompted carefully.

Carl's head turned, eyes narrowing. 'I don't happen to believe that being unable to prove you're innocent automatically means you're guilty. Nobody goes around collecting alibis on the off chance they'll be arrested for murder.'

'No, of course not,' she agreed at once, deciding she would have to tread very warily indeed. 'Er—you must have done a lot of research for the film. I expect you've come up with something more substantial?'

'I think so,' he said blandly.

Eve held her breath. 'That sounds interesting. Are you going to keep it a secret?' She attempted to keep it light.

There was a glint in his eyes, but Eve couldn't tell if it came from within or from the bare electric bulb.

'Not from you when you've been so helpful. You deserve a reward. I call it gut instinct.'

Her eyes flew to his face in consternation. 'That hardly constitutes proof!' she exclaimed in disappointment.

Carl looked down at her in surprise. 'I never said I had proof,' he reminded her softly.

Eve's stomach lurched. Idiot! She'd been racing too far ahead. 'No, but ... I'm afraid I just assumed you had. I guess I was getting overexcited,' she insisted with a faltering laugh.

'And I was just teasing you,' he came back with a laugh. 'Naturally I have proof.'

If he could tease, she could flirt. She pouted reprovingly. 'I see, but you're not going to tell me what it is?'

He smiled appreciatively. 'I haven't made up my mind yet.'

She glanced up at him through her lashes. 'But you might?' she breathed hopefully.

Again he smiled. 'I'll have to think about it.'

Eve managed a sulky tut. 'It's mean of you to tantalise that way. Now I'll never relax until I know.'

This time Carl laughed, watching her in open fascination. 'Bear with me. I've kept it to myself for a long time now. I'd have to weigh the odds. See how worth while it was. You can wait a few hours, can't you?' he insinuated tantalisingly.

Her eyes widened on his face. 'A few hours?' she prompted.

'I'll tell you after dinner what I've decided. That's fair, isn't it?''

Eve forced herself not to get too excited. 'I suppose I can wait that long,' she agreed grudgingly. 'As long as it's worth it,' she amended.

He grinned. 'It will be, I promise. Now, this isn't getting the job done. We'd better get a move on. You go first,' he urged, and the eyes he rested on her back held amusement at her eagerness to obey.

They descended to the next floor and the real work began. Eve made notes until her fingers cramped. Carl knew precisely what he wanted, and by the end of the afternoon his decisions had been made. When they reached the hall again, he took the pad from her.

'Thanks for your help, Eve. I'll get these typed up.'

She smiled. 'I was glad to help.' She meant it too. The whole day had been fascinating. An insight into the real Carl Ramsay. It would actually be very easy to like him if she didn't already hate him so much.

Carl's eyes were glinting again. 'I think it was a profitable afternoon's work,' he pronounced finally, and glanced at his watch. 'Now I must shoot. I've a meeting in ten minutes. I'll see you at dinner. Oh, and don't forget we have that little talk afterwards.'

Eve didn't have to pretend puzzlement because she had actually forgotten, for a moment, all about their rendezvous. It brought a faint colour to her cheeks. 'Oh, yes, that.'

Brows rose. 'That,' he agreed blithely. 'Thanks again, Eve, and you'd better thank Max for the plans, too.' He waved them in a sort of salute and quickly walked away.

Eve stared after him, eyes a triumphant, glittering violet. He was going to tell her, she was sure of it. If his decision had been no, he would scarcely wait to tell her. Once she had the information she could stop having to be pleasant. Though honesty made her admit that that hadn't been such a hardship today. Quite the reverse. In any event, her job would be done. Max would be satisfied. She hoped so. Surely he couldn't ask any more of her?

She was on pins all through dinner that evening. The tension had been building since she went up to change. In a matter of hours it would all be over. There would still be the film, but, if she did as she was told there, Max might let her go. She prayed he would. She honestly didn't know how much more she could take. The strain had been so much worse lately. She was tired of being manipulated and used without thought for her feelings. She wanted her self-respect back before it became irrecoverable.

They were sitting drinking coffee in the lounge, Max presiding over them, directing the flow of conversation as he liked to do, when Carl spoke up.

'If you've no objections, Max, I'd like to whisk Eve away for a while. I have some things I'd like to discuss with her as soon as possible,' he declared with his charming smile.

Eve had said nothing to Max yet, having learned the wisdom of silence the hard way, and she waited to see how he would react to this gambit. He didn't hesitate.

'Of course you may, my dear Carl. I shall have these two lovely ladies to keep me company——' he indicated

Nina and Jenny '—but don't keep her too long. I'm a jealous man where Eve is concerned.'

Carl inclined his head. 'Indeed, as would be any man fortunate enough to possess her. I shall reluctantly return her to you as soon as possible,' he declared gallantly, and rose smoothly, his eyes on Eve.

She hadn't found his words at all amusing, but that didn't show as she rose too. A hand on her arm had her looking down at Max. There was a message in those grey depths that wasn't hard to read—don't forget, I'm counting on you. She managed a tense smile and he released her. Taking a nerve-steadying breath, she passed through the door Carl held for her.

'We'll use the library, I think,' Carl proposed, his hand on her elbow.

That cool touch made her shiver, yet she told herself not to pull away. All she had to do was play these next few minutes right and then it wouldn't matter what she did.

The library was a mellow room, with deep, comfortable leather chairs and couches, made for curling up in with any one of the books that lined the room. Carl went forward to switch on two table-lamps and then turned off the main light. The room was instantly suffused in an intimate glow.

'There, that's more cosy,' he declared in satisfaction. He gave a sideways look to where she stood by the closed door, and strolled to the drinks trolley. 'Brandy?' he queried, reaching for the decanter.

'Not for me,' Eve declined, and watched tensely as he poured a measure for himself.

Taking the glass, Carl sat himself down in one of the deep chairs and crossed his legs, making himself comfortable. 'Come and sit down. You look as if you're poised for flight over there. You've no reason to run away from me, have you?' he queried with some of the old mocking inflection.

Eve moved, aware of his eyes following her as she sank back into a corner of the nearest couch. She waited for him to speak, but he remained silent, watching her as he sipped at the golden liquid. The unwavering regard made her want to squirm, and in order to break it she rose abruptly and walked tensely to the nearest bookcase, examining the contents without seeing anything.

'What's wrong?' Carl asked curiously.

She threw him a glance, but his face was in shadow. 'Nothing. It's just that I thought we came here to talk,' she declared tensely.

'What's the rush?'

Her fingers ran up and down the fine wood of the shelf. 'You heard what Max said. He doesn't like me gone for long.'

Carl set the glass down with a low laugh. 'Max won't mind waiting tonight. However, now that we're here there really isn't much point in wasting time, is there?'

Eve smiled in relief. 'No,' she agreed instantly.

'So, to business. I've changed my mind about tomorrow. As you saw, the crew have got everything set up far quicker than I expected. So there won't be any holiday, we'll start rehearsing instead. You'll have the yellow sheets tonight,' he told her evenly.

She stared at him, stunned. 'That's what you brought me here to tell me?' she gasped unsteadily.

Carl lifted his hand to his chin. 'You were maybe expecting something else?' he asked mildly.

Eve went utterly still. 'You know I was.'

Carl came to his feet with the grace and power of a large jungle cat and prowled towards her. 'Like what?' The question purred from him as he stopped mere inches away.

Eve found herself staring mesmerised into mocking blue eyes as he loomed threateningly over her. 'You said you'd tell me about the proof,' she said thickly, licking her lips.

His brows rose. 'Did I?' he mocked silkily.

'Yes,' she insisted, then faltered. 'That is . . .'

Carl moved, an arm going either side of her as he rested his weight against the shelving, trapping her. 'I remember saying I'd have to see how worth while it would be to tell you. I haven't found out yet. Perhaps you can tell me?' Blue eyes roved over her face, stopping where two pearly teeth fastened on her lip.

Eve gasped, realising finally that she hadn't fooled him for a minute. He had tricked her, leading her up the garden path so skilfully that she had followed like a lamb! Anger surged up inside her, and she raised her hands to his chest to push him away. 'Stop it, Carl. You've had your fun. You've won. Let me go!' It was as futile as trying to knock down a wall with her bare hands.

He laughed tauntingly. 'How can I, when I still don't know?'

Her breathing was laboured with effort and a growing alarm. 'Don't know what?' she asked shakily.

Carl smiled, leaning closer. 'Just how far you're prepared to go to get the information Max wants,' he said softly, and she could feel the warm, brandy-laden brush of his breath on her cheek. He saw the stricken look in her eyes and laughed harshly. 'Did you take me for a fool? Yesterday you hated me—today it was: let's be friends, Carl. You wanted something, and I gave you just enough rope to hang yourself this afternoon.'

'You bastard!' she gasped with loathing, bitter tears of failure making her eyes shine.

Again he laughed. 'That's right. But what are you? You'd do anything for Max, wouldn't you? So let's just see how far that takes you, Eve. You see, if you make it worth my while, I might just tell you, even now. Do you still want to know? Let's find out, shall we?'

Her cry of, 'No!' was drowned under his mouth as his lips crushed down punishingly on hers. Low moans caught in her throat as she tried to push him away with clenched fists, but Carl just caught her fast in his arms, one slipping around her waist, the other going up to her head, his fingers tangling in her hair and holding her head still beneath his.

Throat aching, she kept her lips tightly closed against the barrage, but the need for air defeated her. When she was forced to gasp Carl took instant advantage, lips and tongue claiming her mouth in a dizzying assault. It wasn't rape, but ravishment. One instant she was in control, the next a wave of the most incredible sensation swept through her, dissolving all resistance. She uttered a choked sob. Her hands slowly uncurled and clung as the unfamiliar excitement took hold. She could feel her blood turning thick and hot in her veins, the ultra-sensitive prickling all over her skin as nerve-endings came alive.

Then her mind stopped functioning altogether. Quivering, her body went fluid, melting and moulding against his strong male frame. She sighed achingly, and her tongue met his. The thrill shivered through her from head to foot. Flames flickered deep inside and she felt the surge of her breasts against his chest, so sensitised that it was both a pleasure and a pain. She forgot the who, where and why of it, only knowing a crazy need to experience more of this feeling that had come so abruptly to life.

That made the shock of being thrust so firmly away from the source doubly painful. Confused and disorientated, she raised heavy lids to find herself staring into a mocking, hostile face.

'All the way, Eve? He's got you that hooked?'

Memory returned, freezing her blood. She shuddered, dropping her eyes. But Carl wasn't having that; a harsh hand on her chin forced her head up until she could not avoid him.

'Poor Max, he really must be worried. Unfortunately for him, using you was a bad choice. Tell him that. Anything he wants to know can't be learned that cheaply. All I want from you is your presence on set tomorrow. Got that?'

Swallowing painfully, Eve nodded and he let her go. She sagged back against the shelf, holding on grimly. To fall at his feet would be the final humiliation.

'So thanks, but no, thanks, sweetheart,' he drawled mockingly, using his handkerchief to wipe away any tell-tale lipstick. 'Until tomorrow.'

He left then, closing the door quietly behind him. Eve stared at it for a second, then closed her eyes in pain. She raised one trembling hand to her swollen lips and held back a sob. She had never in her life responded to anyone the way she had to Carl Ramsay tonight. It left her feeling shocked and scared.

Shocked, because it had been Carl doing the kissing. Scared, because she had been totally lost. Completely and utterly lost in him. She had been powerless.

She just couldn't understand how it could have happened. It didn't make sense, and that alarmed her too, because her body told her brain that it didn't need to make sense. It simply was.

Horrified, she crossed unsteadily to the drinks trolley and poured herself the brandy she had refused earlier. It tasted vile, but the warmth coursing through her veins brought back a measure of sanity and control. Relief, too, because Carl hadn't known she was responding to him. He believed she was doing it for Max. Therein lay protection. He didn't know and he would never know. For he would never want to repeat the experiment, believing what he did. So her response—chemistry, pure chemistry—would never be revealed. Everyone knew fires only burned if you fed them, and this one would get no more fuel. It would die—she would be happy to see it in ashes.

As for the rest... Cold rage started to seethe inside her. He had played her for a fool all down the line, and she hated him for it. Hated him for taking away the one small hope she had had of gaining her freedom. It didn't matter that he couldn't have known. He had done it and she wanted to strike out and hurt him. She had the perfect means, too, through his precious film. She would be so appallingly bad he would become a laughing-stock, and then it would be her turn to stand there and crow. She could taste the sweetness of triumph already.

Finishing the drink, she schooled her features into their usual cool mask. She would have to go back and join Max and the others soon. More to the point, she must think of something to tell Max that would keep him partially satisfied. Her heart sank at the thought.

Idly her eyes roved the nearest shelf, focused on one spine, passed on and then returned. *The Maxwell Murder Case* by Rolf Anderson. Eve set the glass down and reached for the book. There were others on the subject alongside it, too, making her realise just how intriguing the case had been over the years. Her fingers traced the gold embossed lettering. Surely Rolf could tell her more about his fiancée Ruth's character than anyone, and she found that she wanted to know, for that sweet face in the portrait was haunting—and innocent.

When she slipped upstairs to repair her make-up, the book went with her.

CHAPTER FIVE

SIGHING, Eve lowered her book, the very one she had taken from the library last night, and marked the page. It was fascinating reading, but she was due somewhere else soon. Actually, she was already ten minutes late, but who was counting? Picking up the coloured pages of script she had found in her room, she grinned. Carl had sent her away to a quiet spot to learn her lines, and she had no intention of telling him he need not have bothered.

What he didn't know was that she had a photographic memory and could recall the lines at will. At school it had been a useful thing to have during exams. It would help her now, if she cared to use it properly. Which she didn't.

She recalled, with a scowl, how intently Carl had watched her with Max at breakfast. He had been wondering what she had reported of the débâcle, and how Max had taken it. In fact, she had hedged successfully, leaving Max with the impression she was making progress slowly. Carl had had nothing to witness.

Glancing at her watch again, she saw that it was half-past two. That ought to be long enough to make him absolutely furious. Coming to her feet gracefully, she made her way unconcernedly downstairs to the conservatory, the scene for today's rehearsals. Everyone turned to look as she came in, but it was Carl her eyes went to.

Clad in thigh-hugging blue jeans, his baggy, short-sleeved shirt open at the neck, he looked intensely, dominatingly masculine. Her errant senses leapt in response despite her will-power. She saw, too, that his dark hair looked as if he had raked impatient fingers through it, and his eyes glittered dangerously.

'I'm sorry I'm late,' she apologised with a rueful smile, threading her way through cables, cameras and lights.

Blue eyes followed her progress. 'Think nothing of it. We've nothing to waste but time and money.' Carl's voice dripped ice.

Eve widened her eyes to their fullest extent. 'I did apologise,' she reminded him coolly.

'Don't you possess a watch?' he queried scornfully. Reaching for her left arm, he held it up. Diamond-encrusted gold glittered. 'I see you do. Cartier's?' He parodied that conversation they had had the first evening.

She lost a little cool at the reminder, and her eyes flashed. 'Van Cleef & Arpels,' she corrected sweetly.

'Naturally,' he mocked, letting her go. 'Well, I trust your tardiness means you're word-perfect. That at least would make the lost time worth while. OK, everybody, now that Eve has deigned to join us, we can get on. Where are you going?' he barked as Eve moved away.

She frowned. 'To sit down.'

He looked her up and down. 'I presume you do intend to take part now that you're here? That being the case, you can stand like the rest of us.'

Eve barely held on to her temper. He knew damn well she hadn't meant that at all. He had absolutely no right to dress her down that way in public. It made her savour what was to come even more.

'Take your places,' Carl called out, and the floor cleared as if by magic. 'Eve, you come with me.' He led her to the door leading into the garden. 'You know your cue? That's something! Right, here's what I want you to do.' With a sudden shift into sheer professionalism that was very impressive, Carl painstakingly outlined the way he saw the scene taking shape.

It was virtually impossible to be anything other than impressed. Carl had shed his personal dislike as if it were a piece of clothing. She realised that, as he had told her mere days ago, he would never let outside influences cloud his judgement in his work. His one aim was to make the best film he could.

She came rather reluctantly to admire his patience at her growing list of mistakes. She missed her cue, or forgot her lines. Managed to get her back constantly to the camera. All icing on the cake of her wooden acting and monotone voice. After the first less than brilliant attempt, he took her aside and repeated his instructions over again. She listened earnestly, giving the impression of wanting to do well, but once again it was a failure.

She became aware of other things than Carl's reaction. At the beginning she had felt a certain sympathy from the other members of the cast, but as the afternoon wore on she saw that gradually fade until all that was left was gloom and despondency. They grew silent, exchanging helpless looks with each other.

Eve knew a moment's compunction then, for scuppering a project they had all had such high hopes of. That was until she looked at Carl and all the reasons to carry on returned full force. There would be other films for them, but only this one for her to achieve her aim.

When Carl finally called it a day, the others left, talking among themselves in low voices. A few called out farewells to her, but the majority viewed her with a variety of emotions, none exactly friendly. Shrugging mentally, she made to leave by the other door.

'Not you, Eve.'

She stopped obediently. Behind a cool front, her eyes sought eagerly for signs of his reaction. She expected anger, and there it was, but something else, too—a deep frustration.

'*That* was a disaster,' he said shortly. 'It seems Max's talk had no effect, after all.'

Her hand went automatically to her cheek, remembering the slap. That was what he thought! 'You can't have what isn't there. I'm doing my best. I never promised to be Katharine Hepburn.'

Carl ran an abstracted hand around his neck. 'I never expected you to be, either. However, I was hoping for more than I got. With what you're giving me, there has to be room for improvement. After dinner, you and I are going to come back here and work on this scene until we get something halfway decent to film.'

Eve's heart gave a great sideways lurch. Being alone with him was something she didn't care for at all. 'That might not be a good idea. You know what Max——'

'Leave Max to me,' he interrupted. 'Now you'd better get over to the wardrobe unit. They need to get started on your costumes or we won't do any filming at all.'

She left, her triumph tempered now by the idea of the coaching lesson to come. She knew that Max would be all for it and she wouldn't be able to argue because that would only lead to revealing things she would rather keep hidden.

Wardrobe and make-up were large, air-conditioned trucks parked in the old stableyard. When Eve stepped up into the former, she found Nina already there being fitted. They exchanged cautious smiles. Eve had found the brunette rather disconcerting with her penetrating eyes, and their contact with each other had been minimal. She got the uncomfortable impression that Nina saw everything.

'How did it go?' she casually asked Eve now.

'Do you mean you couldn't hear the hair tearing out over here?' Eve joked rather diffidently.

Nina laughed. 'Bad as that?' she sympathised.

'Worse! I think we ought to draw a veil over it.'

'Never mind, it's only the first day. You'll get better.'

Eve didn't like the feeling of guilt that the reassurance dredged up, but she could scarcely disagree. 'I hope you're right,' she lied.

The woman who had been busily pinning Nina's dress disappeared into the back of the van, leaving them alone.

'Eve, do you mind if I ask you a personal question? Are you happy with Max?'

The question caught Eve totally by surprise. No one had ever asked her that. Everyone had just assumed. Her throat closed over and she had to cough to clear it in order to speak. 'I wouldn't be anywhere else.'

Nina looked round, reproving. 'That's not what I asked. Oh, never mind. I was being rude. I had no business trying to pry. But I'll just say this, if you'll forgive me. You make a very odd couple. Now I'll shut up.'

Eve pondered that statement long after Nina had gone. What did she see that no one else did? If the mask had slipped, Max would have been the first to tell her. So how had Nina seen that things weren't what they seemed? Eve found it all rather unnerving.

There wasn't much time left before dinner when at last she was free to leave. It made a relaxing bath out of the question, and she had to make do with a shower instead. When she re-entered the bedroom, clad only in her towelling robe, Max was there. She came to an abrupt halt. She hated being near Max when she was barely clothed. He might not touch her, but the eyes he ran over her were lustful. It was hard to resist the urge to check that her belt was securely tied.

'You look tired, my dear.'

'It's been one of those days,' she admitted coolly.

Max smiled. 'So I gather. Carl tells me he needs to rehearse you tonight. I trust his efforts will be no more successful than before?'

Eve crossed her arms. 'If I haven't the talent, no amount of rehearsing will give it to me,' she said flatly.

'Always so sensible, my Eve. Which is good, because I'm going to place a great deal of trust on your common sense,' he told her smoothly.

'What do you mean?' she asked, frowning, and for the first time saw Max put out.

'It really is most inconvenient, but I find I have to go to Geneva. Something has arisen that I had no plans for. My position is such that I have no option but to go.'

'When?'

He came to her then and caught one hand in both of his. 'Tomorrow. Which brings me to you, my dear. I'm certain that our best interests will be foremost in your mind while I'm away, won't they?'

Her free hand clenched. 'Of course. How long will you be gone?'

'I trust that means you'll miss me. However, I cannot put a limit on my absence. I will still expect your reports, my dear. If you make me proud of you, then perhaps I'll have a present for you when I get back.'

Her eyes locked with his. Did he mean the agreement? She could ask, but knew instinctively that he wouldn't tell her. So instead she said, 'I'll do my best.'

He raised her hand to his lips in salute. 'I'm sure you shall. Wear something special tonight, my dear, to wish me *bon voyage*,' he ordered as he left.

She dressed as he wanted in a white silk shift held up by delicate straps, the bodice decorated by swirls of silver thread, but she had even less enthusiasm than usual. His absence should have meant freedom for a week, perhaps even two, yet nothing would be different. She still had to produce the results, and she didn't know how. Except, perhaps, for the film. But she sensed now that its failure wasn't nearly so important to Max as finding out how Carl intended to prove Ruth's innocence.

As soon as dinner was over, Carl excused them both and led the way back to the conservatory. It seemed an alien place at night. Even with the lights on there were dark corners, and shadows thrown by the plants. They rustled, too, as if an unseen presence caught them. Eve told herself not to be so fanciful, for she was edgy enough as it was.

'Right.' Carl shut the door behind them, sealing them into the leafy privacy. 'We'll take it from the top.' He handed her the pages of script. 'You can read it for now. Try to remember you're attempting to seduce Rolf.

You've seen the others go, leaving him in here alone, and you go in.'

Eve took the script, frowning. 'Shouldn't we have Miles here too?' she suggested, wondering why it hadn't occurred to her before.

Carl paused in the process of loosening his tie. 'I'll be reading his part,' he informed her blandly, but his blue eyes challenged her to argue.

After last night, the prospect didn't please at all. How could she argue and avoid revealing it? 'I'd rather Miles was here—after all, he's the one I'm doing the scene with,' she pointed out reasonably.

Carl shot that down easily. 'Miles doesn't need to rehearse, you do. If it's motivation you need, just imagine it's Max you're seducing, with the intention of wheedling a mink or a diamond necklace out of him. That ought to do it.'

Her face tightened angrily. 'You never pass up an opportunity to insult me, do you?' she snapped fiercely.

Carl didn't answer, except to smile cynically at her outrage. He walked away to take up Miles's position. 'When you're ready,' he prompted sardonically. 'Make it some time tonight.'

If she had had a weapon handy, she would gladly have thrust it between his sarcastic shoulder-blades. All she had was the power of her tongue, and she used it to good effect. Moving into the scene, the words left her lips like bullets. She emoted all he could ask for, not seductively, but with a fury.

If Carl hadn't been angry to begin with, he achieved it as the scene progressed. Eve watched it grow, all the more potent for being repressed, her violet eyes glittering with victory. She let him see it was deliberate. She wanted to topple his smug superiority once and for all. He had no right to take a moral stand over her.

When he took her in his arms as the script demanded, they were both soaring on a wave of mutual anger. The kiss was a battlefield in the ongoing war. The need to defeat and dominate of paramount importance.

Seduction had no place here, neither did the film; they had transcended that to the entirely personal. Their lips met, and it was a fierce engagement. Breathing harshly, they sought to conquer the other with bruising kisses. And when neither won, they broke apart, blue eyes locking with violet. The air about them seethed and crackled with an electric charge. Everything went completely and utterly still for a moment in time.

Then Carl uttered a strangulated groan and reached for her, arms drawing her tight into his body with a satisfying rustle of silk. Eve gasped, and at the first brush of his lips every atom of her body took a quantum leap into the unknown and returned again, irrevocably changed. Pleasure took her breath away, and beneath her hands she felt Carl shudder. All power to think and act deserted them as their senses were swamped with wave upon wave of delight.

Another gasp parted her lips. The movement created havoc of the sweetest kind, and she experimented, rubbing them against his. Carl groaned, and fireworks exploded behind lowered lids. The glide of his tongue on the soft inner skin of her lips drowned her in a flood of sensual pleasure.

Her arms found their way around his neck, hands caressing the strong shoulders, drifting up to catch in the silky luxuriance of his hair. With shimmering expertise, his lips were drawing hers to give more and more, and the more she gave, the more they both needed.

His hands moulded her to him, searching out the secret contours as the languorous deepening of their kisses held an eroticism that burnt them in its explosive flames. His taut body was so intimately close to hers that she could feel his wanting of her, and she wanted him, too.

Breathless, they were forced to move away, and the cool air between them brought the world back. The glow in their eyes faded to disbelief. Carl released her as if she burnt him. Face distorted by some inner emotion, he turned away, going to the nearest window and resting his hands on the frame, head lowered.

Eve closed her eyes. Last night only she had felt this; now Carl was part of it, too. And the funniest thing of all was that neither of them wanted it. They despised each other. It could only be a vindictive fate who could deal them this blow.

'I think we'd do well to forget that ever happened.' Carl's voice was bleak and distant.

Eve felt cold. 'Yes,' she agreed. She watched as he stood up and raked his hair with hands that were unsteady. He realised it himself, and examined them, almost in fascination, before thrusting them into his trouser pockets.

They stared at each other uncomfortably, both knowing that to agree to forget was one thing. Carrying it out when they were going to be constantly in each other's company was going to be hard.

'You can forget the scene, we'll be doing another.' He didn't need to explain why, they both knew.

She nodded. 'All right.'

A muscle ticked in his tensed jaw. 'For God's sake, why you?' he exploded.

'Why either of us?' she returned bitterly, and, brushing past him, let herself out of the room.

The sound of a car engine fading away down the drive stirred Eve just after dawn. Max had gone. Tiredly she rubbed her eyes. She hadn't been sleeping; she hadn't slept all night. Her brain had kept going over and over that passionate encounter with Carl.

She sat up, oppressed by this new cross to bear. The early sunlight coming in the window gave her a little warmth, and suddenly she knew that what she wanted most was fresh air. Clean bright air, with no Max and no Carl. Flinging back the covers, she padded into her dressing-room. From the back of one wardrobe, hidden

by the butterfly hues of her evening gowns, she drew a
faded pair of jeans, a baggy sweatshirt and a pair of
running shoes. She used them only when Max was away,
because if he had known of their existence he would have
burnt them.

Donning them quickly, leaving her hair flowing loose
around a bare face, she gathered up Rolf Anderson's
book and used the back stairs to reach the ground floor,
quietly letting herself out via the kitchen. It was freedom
of a sort, and she set off across the lawns towards the
woodland that hid the shore from view.

Max never came down to the rocky shoreline. It was
too rough and wild for his aesthetic tastes. Knowing that
his presence didn't linger here lifted the weight from her
shoulders for a while. She walked until she found a com-
fortable-looking rock sheltered from the breeze, and
propped herself against it.

Opening the book upon her knees, she started to read
on. Ruth Maxwell had been convicted because she had
had the opportunity, having been alone in the house with
her father. The motive—the exact amount of money her
father had been known to have in his wallet—was found
in her jewel case. Henry was known to keep his family
short of cash, and Ruth hadn't been able to explain how
the money got there. Her fingerprints had also been on
the murder weapon—a poker. She had admitted using
it the day before, but it was summer and there were no
fires in the house. Those were the points the prosecution
case had rested on. Little attention had been paid to the
fact that Henry had also been stripped of a diamond
tie-pin and a distinctive ruby ring—neither of which had
been found in Ruth's possession.

As Carl had said, she hadn't been able to prove she
was innocent, but it didn't make her guilty—except in
the eyes of the jury.

Eve stretched. The sun had risen higher. It must be
getting near breakfast-time. She would have to go back.
She closed the book with a sigh of regret and stood up.

The water looked inviting, but she had no costume. Instead she took off her shoes and hung them around her neck by their laces, rolled up her jeans, and paddled her way back up the beach.

Level with the house, she stopped, staring dejectedly out to sea. She was reluctant to go back. Sometimes she felt as if she couldn't breathe in the house. But she knew she had to go, for she had a job to do. She couldn't risk not doing it and having the resultant publicity expose her mother to the world. She turned and slowly made her way up the sand.

Before she entered the woods again, she stopped to dust off her feet and put her shoes back on, then, picking up the book, she carried on her way. It was cool and green and shady under the trees. That was why she didn't see the figure as she rounded a bend in the path until it was too late.

Gasping in shock, she stepped backwards instinctively, and overbalanced. The book flew from her grasp to lie forgotten as Carl's hands shot out to steady her and save her from falling.

Blue eyes scanned her face closely. 'You look tired,' he observed, then, realising he was still holding her, he released her slowly.

'So do you,' she responded, feeling the atavistic rise of the hairs on her body at his unexpected nearness, so soon after last night.

They both faced each other tensely then, because the reason for the sleeplessness was obvious. As if drawn, Carl's eyes dropped to run over her casually dressed figure before meeting her eyes again.

'Does Max know what you get up to when he's away?' he asked, and his voice was husky and unwittingly sensual.

Eve shivered. While she knew she ought to leave, somehow she couldn't make her legs obey. She swallowed. 'No, and I'd rather he didn't.'

One eyebrow rose. 'Secrets?'

She was over the shock, but her heart hadn't settled down at all. 'I like to let my hair down occasionally, but Max prefers me to look...'

'Beddable?' he suggested, when she was lost for a word. 'Funny, you look far more desirable like this, with your hair mussed and your cheeks flushed.'

Her stomach clenched painfully. 'Carl! You're forgetting who I am!' she implored in a voice that shook.

A nerve started to tic in his jaw. 'I wish to God I could! I wish I could say to hell with who and what you are and just take you!'

She gasped. 'And do you imagine I'd simply let you?' she demanded, choked and angry, because the visions he aroused were a torch to her senses.

His eyes were almost black. 'Yes. If I touched you...' He reached out a hand towards her.

'Don't!' she ordered faintly.

Carl dropped his hand, face now pale and tense. 'Dear God, I disgust myself. To want something Max has had before me!'

The pain that caused was unbelievable. 'Do you think I'm proud of *myself*, knowing you despise me?' she challenged vehemently.

The silence was thick and churning with emotion between them.

'But it doesn't stop the wanting, does it?' he stated hoarsely.

Eve closed her eyes. 'No,' she admitted, because to lie was useless. It was there. As apparent and vital as it had once seemed impossible. 'I'd better go,' she said, looking away from him.

'Yes,' he agreed, but as she moved to go around him his hand shot out to catch her arm. Her eyes shot to his, wide and alarmed. The tension on Carl's face was awesome. 'I think I must,' he murmured huskily, drawing her closer.

Eve started to tremble. 'Please!' It was barely a groan as his mouth lowered to hers, and she didn't know if she was begging him to stop or go on.

Passion exploded instantly as their lips clung and parted, allowing their tongues to meet in a sensual dance of mutual pleasure. No other part of them touched, and yet it felt as if she had been taken over completely. It was wonderful, but crazy and futile and hopelessly destructive.

She dragged her lips from his and uttered one choked word. 'Max.'

Carl went still, and when she looked at him she saw the anger and loathing—and something she knew simply couldn't be defeat. 'Go!' he ordered abruptly. 'For God's sake, just go.'

Eve went, stumbling at first on her shaky legs, but finally finding the strength to run towards the house as if her life depended on it.

Behind her, Carl thudded one fist hard against the nearest tree, grateful for the pain of it. Then, as he turned, he saw the book that Eve had dropped. Bending, he retrieved it and turned it over. The title made him draw in his breath in surprise. It set him back on his heels, and the eyes he turned on the path she had taken were deeply thoughtful.

It wasn't easy, over the next few days, to pretend that nothing had happened. Eve tried, but the knowledge was always there. Her senses seemed to have been heightened to a fine point of awareness. She 'felt' Carl, even across a room, and being close to him in the demands of their work was a refinement of torture to her senses.

Carl was so cool, so remote, she was certain she alone suffered these new agonies, until they touched accidentally and she found her anxious gaze locked with a devouring blue one. Hastily though he hid it, Eve now knew that she wasn't alone. Yet she was as unwilling as he to feel this—excitement. By unspoken consent they took to avoiding each other unless absolutely necessary.

She welcomed his deepening coldness due to her acting—or rather the lack of it—willing this fever of the blood to die quickly and end her confusion. For she was confused, desperately. She needed to hate Carl, but it just wasn't there. Something more potent was taking its place. Something she couldn't fight—and that scared her.

Not only that, but she was suffering a crisis of conscience, too. Her determination to damage the film had faltered, leaving only Max's orders. But she couldn't reconcile those with her growing conviction that Ruth Maxwell was innocent, and that the film ought to be allowed to say so. She was beginning to care, quite deeply, and she couldn't afford to.

So, all in all, it was a very shaken woman who watched the last member of the cast arrive on Saturday. Harvey Logan was a character actor of some repute. Tall and well built, with a shock of silver-grey hair, he had that true presence given only to few. Eve had seen him many times in films and admired him enormously. Under normal circumstances, it would be a delight to have him play Velda's husband, Henry Maxwell.

He arrived late in the afternoon, brimming over with *joie de vivre*, and sporting a tan that flattered his looks and showed that his last enterprise had been filmed in more exotic climes.

Eve, a spectator, watched as the scene being filmed was abruptly cut and Carl went forward, smiling, to greet the newcomer. Soon the two men were surrounded by a group of welcoming cast and crew, all greeting Harvey Logan with affection.

When the first rush was over, Carl drily ordered a break, which made everyone laugh. Slowly they drifted from the house towards the refreshment van, leaving the two men alone. Feeling as if she was intruding, Eve decided she should leave too. Unfortunately her movement in the virtually empty room drew both men's attention.

'Colleen?'

The sharp-voiced query brought Eve to an appalled standstill. She found Harvey Logan staring at her in blank astonishment.

'As I live and breathe, it's Colleen MacManus!' he declared in delight.

Eve paled. Never had she dreamed that she would meet anyone who had known her mother. The likeness between the two of them hadn't seemed a threat. Now, danger signals flashed inside her head. She had to think fast. Her lips framed an apologetic smile. 'I'm so sorry, but you've mistaken me for someone else. I'm not...who did you say?' She held out her hand to ward off his patent intention to sweep her into his arms.

Harvey Logan paused mid-stride, shook his head, laughed, and captured her hand. 'No, I can see that. You're too young, and I was forgetting the lovely lady died. What a sad day that was.'

Groaning inwardly, Eve tried again, eyes flicking to Carl's stony face and away again. 'Yes, but...I'm trying to tell you——' She got no further, for the older man was irrepressible.

'You must be little Evie.' He smiled warmly. 'Your mother was always talking about you, showing us pictures your father sent her. There couldn't have been a prouder woman. Damn, but you're the image of her. Come and give us a hug. I've felt like your uncle all your life!'

Willy-nilly, Eve was swept into a warm embrace, and suddenly her throat and eyes were choked with emotional tears. Here was someone who had loved her mother, a shared bond, and keeping the truth of her mother's supposed death from him seemed like treachery. When Harvey set her on her feet again, she gazed up at him, violet eyes moist, as were his.

'Let me look at you. It's like seeing a ghost!' He shook his head again.

Eve breathed in deeply, recognising that pretence was pointless now. 'You knew my mother?' she asked faintly.

'We were on stage together more times than I can remember. The stage was my first love, as it was Colleen's,' he declared reminiscently.

'Yes,' she agreed, smiling. 'She was never the same away from it. She had to go to it. She had no choice.'

Harvey laid an arm across her shoulders. 'Ah, so you saw it too. Your father knew. He was a wise man. He knew that sometimes loving someone means letting them go.'

Eve sighed. 'I used to feel sorry for him, until I realised that making Mum happy was happiness enough for him. And now——' She broke off, realising just how indiscreet she was about to be.

'And now,' Harvey went on, 'he's readjusting to your taking after her.'

Brought up short, Eve found herself staring into Carl's inimical eyes. Faint colour entered her cheeks as she shook her head. 'I'm afraid not.'

Harvey's surprise was patent. 'But you're here, honey,' he pointed out the obvious.

Carl chose that moment to enter the lists, his voice silky. 'She's here because this is Max's house, and she lives with Max.'

Harvey could scarcely believe it. 'You mean . . . ?'

Eve quietly disengaged herself as Carl nodded. 'Precisely.'

The older man sobered quite considerably. When he looked at Eve now, there was disappointment in his eyes and she knew that she had sunk in his estimation. It made her feel cold inside. 'I'm sorry to hear that, Evie; your mother would be too.'

That was a very low blow and she flushed painfully, tilting her chin. 'I'm not about to apologise to anyone for the way I live my life. I'd like to talk to you about my mother, Mr Logan, but only if you save yourself the trouble of trying to save me from myself. I'm a grown woman. I know what I'm doing.'

'Such as trying to be a star like your mother without one scrap of the talent!' Carl scorned. 'Getting Max to buy you into this film was the only way, wasn't it? That's quite a novel twist to the casting-couch route.'

Eve flinched at his bringing the fight into the open this way. Her eyes clashed violently with his. 'Oh, indeed,' she drawled. 'And we both know how un-tempted you are to follow the same route...don't we?'

Carl took a hasty step forwards. 'If you weren't a wo-man—— ' he began, and then controlled himself.

'You'd what? Hit me?' she demanded passionately. 'Hit me and then...' She saw his face and it wasn't angry, but stark with a tension that she felt too. She drew in a ragged breath. They had both gone too far. 'Oh, God, I hate you!' she cried, brushing hastily between them, leaving them staring after her.

The library was the closest room, and Eve shut herself in there. She was still shaking badly. It was frightening how quickly their emotions could erupt. The feelings they had revealed to Harvey made her cringe. How could he have done it? How could she?

Eve crossed to the nearest chair and sat down, closing her eyes wearily. No sooner had she done so, than she heard the door click open and shut. By the sudden tension in the air, she knew precisely who had come in.

'Why didn't you tell me who you were?' Carl de-manded harshly.

'What difference would it have made?' she countered agitatedly.

'It would have made me feel less a fool!' he snapped back.

Eve sat up and glared at him. 'I can't be responsible for how you feel. If it helps I'll apologise, but we both know it changes nothing,' she returned tiredly.

Carl pushed himself away from the door and came to lean over her. She recoiled instantly, nerves jangling.

'Maybe it does,' he said softly. 'Can it be possible, I ask myself, that the famed Colleen MacManus's daughter can't act?'

This was what she was afraid of. 'Yes,' she bit out unevenly. 'It's entirely possible. Or don't you believe the evidence of your own eyes?'

'My eyes tell me——' he began harshly, then something made him stop and say in an altogether different tone, 'How can the woman who lives with a man like Max see her parents' love for each other so clearly?'

Her nerves leapt. 'What?' The question was an aching whisper.

His anger was gone, but a fine tension remained—growing. 'It doesn't compute,' he stated huskily as the air thickened and churned about them.

Eve swallowed. 'You're talking nonsense.'

'Am I?'

'Yes,' she confirmed, and her tongue appeared to moisten her lips.

Carl dropped his eyes. 'Have you any idea how erotic that is?'

Eve went still. Afraid to speak, afraid to move. He was like a magnet, drawing her. It was mind-blowing that she felt exhausted by the strain of sitting in the chair. She didn't know what was happening, hardly recognised herself any more. A second ago they had been fighting—and now... Her eyes fell to his throat. Beneath the tanned skin, a pulse beat raggedly. Without conscious volition her hand rose to touch it. His skin was like silk under her fingers. Hot and smooth.

She had never experienced such an intense desire to explore the male body as she did in that moment. But not just any body—only Carl's. It made her heart beat faster and dried her mouth. She didn't remember moving, or even that he reached for her too, she only knew that she was on her feet and in his arms, and her lips had taken the place of her fingers. Her tongue darted out, tasting him, and against her ear Carl groaned.

She realised some of her own power then, and the thrill of it was almost as great as the touch of his hands on her back as he eased her blouse from her skirt. His lips burned her throat up to her ear, and her head fell back helplessly, eyes closing as he tipped her until he could reach her own frantically beating pulse. Then she felt the cool brush of air as her blouse was pushed aside and his hand closed possessively over her breast.

Her soft cry arrested him, and he lifted his head, gazing down at her, blue eyes almost black with emotion. 'What are you doing to me?' His voice was pained.

Eve couldn't speak, could only shake her head.

His fingers tightened unconsciously. 'How many have there been, Eve? How many fools like me have you caught in your net to make life with Max more bearable?'

She simply couldn't believe he had said that. Her face broke up painfully as he stared at her. 'That's a foul thing to suggest!'

'Is it?' he challenged thickly. 'God! You've got me so screwed up that I don't know any more. Sometimes I think I'm losing my mind.'

'I never asked for this. You know that!' she whispered with painful honesty.

'Maybe you did, maybe you didn't. The fact is it's here, and we have two choices.'

Eve's heart stopped. 'What choices?'

Carl smiled grimly. 'Either we go on as we are, pretending it doesn't exist—or we accept it and enjoy it while it lasts.'

Why that should shock her she had no idea, but it did. 'You mean, have an affair?' It wasn't the moral issue that alarmed her, but the knowledge that she didn't want an affair with Carl.

The passion in his eyes turned to mockery. 'Would it be so terrible?'

She answered from the heart. 'Yes . . . Yes, it would.'

He let her go, lip curling. 'Perhaps you're right. Instant satisfaction is no return for long-term self-disgust.'

Eve flinched as if he had struck her. He had misunderstood and she was glad now that he had, but before she could strike back there was a knock on the door.

'Carl? Are you in there?' It was Miles, followed by his hand on the door-handle.

Carl reacted instantly. Eve was twisted away behind him and he crossed to the door in three quick strides, blocking the young man's view into the room in the nick of time.

'What is it, Miles?' His voice was back to normal, too.

'Oh—er—we're all waiting,' the young actor reported lamely.

'I'll be there in a minute,' Carl promised, and shut the door.

Eve finished buttoning her blouse and pushed it into her skirt, using the time to compose herself before facing him. Apart from his pale face, nobody could tell that anything had happened.

'What do you want me to say?' he asked without inflection.

He had said quite enough already. 'Nothing. Nothing at all. Hadn't you better go? You're wanted,' she said coldly.

Still Carl hesitated. 'Eve...' His fist thudded into the wood. 'Damn you!' he bit out harshly, and went, banging the door behind him.

Eve dropped her head in her hands and cried. Oh, God, what was she going to do? She had the awful premonition that this attraction was stronger than either of them had expected, and she didn't know how she was going to cope with that.

CHAPTER SIX

EVE was alone in the lounge on Sunday evening when Nina came in. She was surprised, for Harvey had taken Nina and the others in to Boston for dinner, and she hadn't expected them back for hours. She had been invited herself, but had been glad of the excuse of waiting for Max's call to refuse. In a restaurant there would have been nowhere for her to go to avoid Carl, and that had become even more of a priority since yesterday.

'Hi.' Nina's greeting was a little less reserved than it had been of late. Despite her reservations about Eve's part in the film, she saw no reason not to be moderately friendly. She had the impression that Eve could do with some friends. 'Did Max ring?' she asked, and pursed her lips slightly at the way Eve's face closed up.

'Yes.'

Nina perched herself on the arm of the couch. 'He never misses, does he? What it is to have someone care like that!' She made the remark teasing, but her eyes were astute. Eve, surprisingly, shivered.

'How was the meal?' Eve's smile was strained.

Nina rolled her eyes. 'Exactly what you'd expect of the Hyatt Regency. Expensive, delicious and depressingly fattening,' she joked, and was relieved to see the other woman laugh naturally. 'I come, actually, as the bearer of a message,' she added. 'Carl wants you down in the projection room.'

The laughter was wiped from Eve's face and her stomach knotted. It had been doing that ever since that crying jag yesterday. She still didn't know why she had wept so brokenly and for so long.

'Oh. Do you know why?' She could feel the tension growing already.

Nina pulled a face. 'Not exactly, though I imagine it's something to do with the rushes.'

Eve had known that Carl used Max's small cinema every evening for that purpose, but she had never been invited to see them. Until now.

'Have you seen them?'

'I've just come from there.' Nina smiled apologetically.

Eve sighed, raising a hand to rub her temple. 'They're bad, aren't they?' Why should that depress her? They were supposed to be!

'Not very good,' the brunette admitted with reluctant honesty. 'But anybody can see you're trying your best,' she added.

Now Eve felt guilty. 'Is he angry?'

'It's not always easy to tell with Carl. My guess is he's just defeated. He had such high hopes. It's not easy seeing them go down the drain.'

Sighing, Eve rose gracefully to her feet and went to the door. There she paused and glanced back at Nina. 'I know you all think I ought to give up, let someone better take over, but this is my only chance.'

Nina shrugged. 'I won't judge you, even if I don't approve. Whatever you do must be your decision. You know what's right and just. If you ignore it, then you live with it.'

Eve nodded and left before she was tempted to unburden herself to the brunette. That was a luxury she couldn't allow herself. With a marked degree of reluctance, she made her way down into the basement to the viewing-room.

Carl was sitting in one of the chairs, feet up and chin sunk upon his chest. At first she thought he hadn't heard her entrance, but then he spoke.

'Glad you could make it,' he drawled cuttingly, a tone she had become accustomed to in the last twenty-four hours. That last scene in the library had deteriorated their relationship until they were barely talking at all. 'Take a seat,' he offered, then raised his voice, 'OK, Wilf, run it through again.'

Eve had barely sat down when the lights dimmed and the screen flickered to life. She had never seen rushes before, and watched in interest until her own scenes suddenly appeared before her. They were excruciatingly awful. Max would have been proud of them. Eve would have given a great deal to simply get up and leave, but she couldn't. She watched it through to the bitter end, tension mounting with every second.

When the screen went blank and the lights came up, she kept her eyes looking straight ahead.

Carl raised his voice again. 'That's all for tonight, thanks, Wilf,' he dismissed the invisible projectionist, and only then gave her his attention. 'I'd be interested to hear your comments,' he said levelly.

Eve cleared her throat. 'They're pretty bad,' she admitted.

'And?'

'I'm sorry.' What else could she possibly say? Certainly not, 'Forgive me,' even if that was what she wanted to say.

Carl laughed caustically. '*You're* sorry? I'm the one who's sorry, sweetheart, for ever having allowed myself to get into this mess. I guess it goes to show that you shouldn't want anything too much,' he finished, sounding unutterably weary.

Eve twisted to face him then. He wasn't looking at her, his head was tipped back as he stared up at the ceiling. 'I don't follow you.'

'You aren't required to. The question remains: are you serious enough about your wish to act, to help me improve this film?' he outlined flatly.

Eve suddenly found herself in a minefield, and it would pay to step very carefully. 'How?'

Without glancing at her, Carl explained. 'Max and I have a contract as regards you. It was drawn up six months ago when he agreed to let me use the house for the film. In it is one vitally interesting clause. It says that should you at any time choose to leave the film, I have to let you go. The onus being on your wanting to go.'

Eve sat there, frozen, suddenly seeing everything very clearly. Max had never wanted her for his mistress at all. He had wanted her solely to ruin Carl's film. He had made that deal with Carl before he'd even known she existed! She, innocent fool, had walked into his life at the precise moment he'd needed her—a victim and a tool made to order. If it hadn't been her, it would have been somebody else—someone whom he could blackmail into doing what he wanted. He had planned that clause, and planned that Carl would be forced to ask her to leave, sooner or later. He had also planned that she could never ask to be released.

Dear God, what sort of monster was he? Her loathing for that evil, devious mind swelled to choke her.

Beside her, Carl was waiting. She wanted to beg him not to go on, not to put them both through this torture. But he knew nothing, and, sick at heart, she knew she could do nothing to stop Max's plan from reaching its conclusion.

Throat tight and aching, she forced her lips to frame the word that would bring the walls crashing down. 'So?' she asked, and heard the trap close.

'I want you to tell Max you want out.' Carl's own loathing of being forced was in the absence of all emotion from his voice.

Eve couldn't look at him. 'I don't want to leave the film,' she declared with husky finality.

Carl looked at her then for the first time. 'So, you don't want to help?'

It was all she could do to hold his contemptuous gaze steadily. She felt dirty. 'I don't want to leave the film,' she insisted.

'Then I'll have to find a way to persuade you,' he declared purposefully.

Couldn't he see how hopeless it was? Max had them exactly where he wanted them! Casting aside his pride to appeal to her was so pointless. Carl didn't deserve this and she hated seeing it. Her despair made her angry and the only one she could turn it on was him. Just wishing she could stop him, her eyes clashed angrily with his. 'You can't,' she said with utter finality.

His face closed up. 'Let me be the judge of that,' he advised icily.

Meeting his unswervable determination, Eve sat back, crossing her arms. 'OK, go ahead. I can't stop you wasting your time,' she declared belligerently.

'I won't be if I appeal to the woman who thinks Ruth was innocent. The woman who knows that love has no limitations,' he asserted softly, making her head dart round again as if it were on strings. 'Whatever turned you into what you are, that woman exists inside you still. I'm hoping she'll listen.

'I didn't intend to reveal anything of this, but you've forced my hand. Perhaps you'll understand when I tell you my full name is Carl Anderson Ramsay. Rolf was my grandfather. He loved Ruth very much and never believed she was guilty. Only he could never prove it. I don't think he ever forgave himself for that. He tried for years, though, collecting all the statements, trial transcripts. Anything and everything. He hoped to get the authorities to realise that a miscarriage of justice had occurred, but they just weren't interested. The case remained closed.'

He paused then, as if feeling his grandfather's disheartenment. 'Anyway, eventually he found a decent, loving woman and married her, as Ruth had wanted him to, and they had a daughter, my mother. Grandfather had had to put aside his work on the case, but he never entirely forgot it. As you know, he wrote that book. But it wasn't until I came along and showed an interest that he passed over all his papers to me and asked me to do something about it.

'It became as much of an obsession with me, too. But after all this time I doubted that anyone would really care, unless I brought it to a wider audience. It became a matter of principle to turn the case into a film. You could call it a labour of love. And so, when I finally managed to persuade Max to let me use the house, I thought my chance had come. Until he told me about you. You were part of the deal and I had no choice but to accept you.

'I've told you why this film is important to me, why it had to be good. I'm doing it for my grandfather, for Ruth. Because she was innocent, and you know it too. Get out of the film, Eve. If acting is important to you, I'll get you into another film, but not this one.' His final appeal was issued with a husky emotionalism perhaps even he hadn't intended.

Eve listened in sick despair. Now she understood why Carl had been willing to accept any deal to come here. He had a mission—a mission of love for his grandfather. The trouble was that, however much she wanted to help him, and she did, for Ruth's sake, she simply couldn't. She was going to have to refuse again, and she could never tell him why, or that his tale hadn't fallen on deaf ears. She was glad he had told her, but oh, God, how she wished he hadn't, for now her position was even more intolerable.

Her mind flew to Max. Carl didn't know just how badly Max wanted the film to fail. But why did he? Out of spite? No, it went deeper, and suddenly she had to know.

'Why do you and Max hate each other?'

Carl shot her a sideways look. 'Is that relevant?'

Eve turned on him a face pale with strain. 'Please, Carl, I have to know.'

Carl's face hardened. 'Very well. Because Max is Velda Maxwell's son,' he revealed shockingly.

Eve couldn't hide her gasp. 'Velda's son?' And then she wondered why she had never seen how alike his eyes and mouth were to Velda's in the portrait. But if it was true, and she didn't really doubt it, it only made the mystery darker. 'But why did he let you come here? Why let you make the film at all?' she asked incredulously.

Carl laughed without humour. 'Because he knows that I've always believed the evidence that would have cleared Ruth was hidden somewhere in the house. The film was an excuse, in a way, to get me here, to allow me to look. Because he knows that if such evidence exists, and he would never admit it did, I'll never find it. He wanted to see what I would do. To Max, that was the supreme amusement.'

Oh, yes, she could see that so very clearly now. 'Dear God!' The whole thing appalled her.

Carl sensed he had her on his side now, and he pressed home his advantage. 'Max is using your ambition, Eve. Your presence in the film gives him a control over me. But he's forgetting that clause. If you really believe Ruth was innocent, you'll take that way out.'

Eve could feel her colour draining away. It was like a nightmare. There *was* no way out and Max knew it! Carl was asking for the impossible and she couldn't bear to hear any more!

'I have to think!' she cried distractedly, pushing herself to her feet.

Carl moved like lightning to catch her wrist. 'What's to think about? You know the whole of it now. I'll see you don't lose out. You have to agree!' he declared forcefully.

Eve pulled herself free with a superhuman effort. 'Everything's so clear-cut to you, isn't it, Carl? Black or white, no grey. Don't you think that if it was really that easy I would be agreeing now?' she charged vehemently.

His face hardened to stone. 'All right, how much is it going to cost me?'

She gasped as the pain of that cut her to the quick. 'I can't be bought!' she snapped witheringly.

Carl's laughter wasn't pleasant. '*You* can't be bought? What the hell do you think Max is doing?' Before she could move away, his hand had closed on the diamond drop that glittered at her throat. 'This buys you, sweetheart. It tells the whole world your price.'

Her anger broke all bounds. 'You stupid, conceited fool! You know nothing! You're like a child, blind to everything but its own empty stomach! Well, grow up, Carl, and join the real world. Until you do, for God's sake leave me be!'

White-lipped and angry, he stared at her, then some of the desperation she was feeling must have reached him because suddenly he let her go. She stared at him speechlessly for one second longer, then, with a gasp, turned and hurried to the door. Once outside, she ran. She didn't stop running until she was inside her room and could throw herself down on to the bed.

Her brain was buzzing with all she had learned tonight. Her emotions were being torn in so many directions. Hatred of Max for treating them like pawns. Anger at Carl for trying to manipulate her too. She wanted to help Ruth and Rolf, but not at the expense of her mother. There was just no way she could leave the film. Max had made certain, all those months ago, that she had to keep the part.

Then from the depths of her despair a gleam of an idea flashed across her mind, and she gasped, blinking, trying to hold on to it. Yes, she had to stay, but with Max away how would he know if she was good or bad? She sat up, hands rubbing at thumping temples. What had Max said tonight? There was trouble in Geneva, it could take weeks to sort out. Weeks. What could they achieve in that time? Dear God, if the crew were to leave before Max returned, he need never know. She could tell him it was bad and he would believe her. By the time he learned differently, surely she would be free of him?

Eve chewed on her lip. It was a risk. Dared she take it? So many things could go wrong. But she wanted to.

She was so tired of being used. And it would show Carl that she wasn't the selfish bitch he thought her to be.

Quite why that should be so important, she didn't know.

Deep in thought, her anger forgotten, Eve padded into the bathroom and drew a long, hot bath. Lying back in the scented water, she worked out the details with a growing feeling of being in control of her own life at last. That night she slept like a log and awoke to a new sense of determination. It could be done and she knew precisely *how* she was going to do it.

Eve found it ironic to realise that the scene they were to shoot first that day was the very one they had started with a week ago, and which Carl had shelved after that passionately explosive encounter in the conservatory. The memory raised the tiny hairs on her flesh, making her shiver. Would he be remembering too? Her heart thudded and she pushed the thought away. What did it matter anyway? Anyone would think she wanted it to happen again, and that was ridiculous. Absolutely ridiculous!

After breakfast, a meal of toast and coffee taken in her room, she took herself off to make-up and wardrobe, an odd feeling of detachment surrounding her. Her thoughts were concentrated so fully on the scene that the rest of the world had an unreality about it.

Everything was set up in the conservatory when she returned in costume, her make-up making her every inch the flapper. She was nervous, but in a way that made the adrenalin pump through her. As the last-minute flurry of activity took place around her, she stood to one side psyching herself into the role, something she had never attempted to do before.

Then Carl was before her, his face pale and strained, as if he hadn't slept. 'You weren't at breakfast,' he said shortly, eyes running critically over her appearance.

'I had something in my room.'

His eyes caught hers. 'I had the strange idea you were avoiding me,' he drawled sardonically.

He was right, too—she hadn't wanted to see him, for a variety of reasons. Admitting it, though, was a different matter. 'Why should I?'

Carl's lips curled. 'Because you knew what I intended to ask you. Did you think it over?'

She sighed. 'Yes, and nothing has changed. I won't ask to leave the film, Carl.' She would have said more, but wasn't allowed to.

'You little bitch! You really don't care for anything but yourself, do you?' Somehow it was much worse for not being shouted. Carl raked a hand through his hair and laughed without humour. 'I don't need to go over this scene, do I? I'd only be wasting my time. Just look on it as a monument to your ego and do your best,' he finished sarcastically, and walked away.

For a second she was tempted to change her mind, but only for a second. This was for Ruth, not Carl. She would do her best despite how angry he made her.

She waited for her cue, took her first steps, and everything fell into place. As she walked into the conservatory she wasn't Eve Hunter, but Velda Maxwell. There was seduction in every move of her body, in every changing expression on her face. Miles reacted to it like someone star-struck, as perhaps Rolf would have been in reality. She seduced, and the whole scene came alive. Nobody dared to breathe as they witnessed that transformation from ugly duckling to swan. The very air crackled with suppressed excitement.

When at last Carl called, 'Cut' the silence was deafening. Miles eased them out of the passionate kiss they had been sharing, his expression doubtful. As she turned round to face Carl, she encountered various degrees of emotion from surprise to anger. Nina, though, looked concerned, and so did Harvey. Then she met Carl's eyes and found them blazing in a chalk-white face.

Like everyone else, it was his reaction she waited for. That his fury was held on a very short leash was evident to all. He virtually exploded out of his chair to catch her arm in a vice-like grip. Uncaring of the onlookers, he dragged her from the room. She was pulled, stumbling after him, up the stairs and along to his room, where he thrust her inside, slamming and locking the door after him. The force of his push staggered her over by the bed. Catching her balance, she faced him, at bay.

'I wanted to explain,' she said uneasily as he advanced on her menacingly.

'Explain what? That you're a spiteful little bitch who's been wasting my time and everybody else's for the past week?' he demanded aggressively. 'What were you waiting for, or do I know? Now you can tell Max what he wants to know. How was he going to reward you? What a shame he isn't here, but perhaps I can think of something suitable for today's magnanimous little gesture.'

The glitter of malice in his eyes made her blood run cold. Reading his intent there made her afraid for the first time. She had pushed him too far. 'Don't touch me!'

'Why not?' he jeered. 'It's what you want. What you've always wanted.' His hands reached for her, and she tried to swat them away, without success.

'Carl, don't!' she pleaded in a hoarse voice, but it was drowned beneath his mouth.

Eve tried to fight him, but he was too strong for her, too angry. His weight bore her backwards on to the bed, where he pinned her down as his mouth ravaged hers remorselessly. She felt cold and sick in her helplessness. Pained tears clogged her throat and eyes. His hands were everywhere, without gentleness, his caresses insulting. As his lips left hers to plunder her neck, she sobbed, and the tears spilt over.

Then his roving lips encountered the wetness on her cheeks and he froze. Lifting his head, he saw the shock of fear in her white face, and the tears flooding her eyes. Without a word he rolled off her on to his back, one arm covering his eyes, chest heaving. Limp with relief, Eve rolled over too, burying her head in her arms, sobbing weakly.

'God!' Carl uttered disbelievingly. 'I never meant to... How do you always manage to incite me into losing all control?' he finished, swallowing hard.

Eve didn't answer. Her sobs had died, leaving her shivering and weak.

'Why?' he asked, a second or two later.

It was a multi-layered question that he didn't need to clarify. She knew them all. She would answer what she could, but she still had to protect herself.

'You asked me to help you with the film,' she sighed, voice low and husky. 'Well, I won't leave it, because it's important to me. I decided to stop pretending instead. I know, you want to know why I was doing it. You know the answer. All the things you said to me. I had to pay you back. That's all, so don't ask me any more questions. I've said all I'm going to. It's all you want. For Ruth and your grandfather. But I have to ask you to promise me something.' She felt the movement of the bed as Carl sat up and turned to gaze down at her.

'And that is?' he growled.

'You and Max are enemies, with me in the middle. I don't want him to know that I'm helping you. I—don't want to lose what I have here, or Max. We have to finish before he returns. If you can't promise me that, then it will have to be the way it was,' Eve declared as levelly as she could. The next thing she knew strong hands were turning her over. She had bare seconds in which to school her features into a cool mask.

Carl's eyes were penetrating. 'What game are you playing now?'

'It's no game. I'm just telling you the way it is.'

'Is Max more important than the talent you have? You can believe me when I tell you the world could be your oyster. So why stay here?'

Eve averted her eyes and sat up. He was getting too close. 'Because Max gives me something no one else can, and I want it. I won't give it up for anyone or anything. I gave you a choice, take it or leave it,' she ordered frigidly.

Carl's face was a mixture of incredulity and contempt. 'Do I have a choice?' he drawled nastily. 'You're a prize, Eve Hunter, a real prize, and Max is welcome to you.'

She smiled thinly, righting her beleaguered dress. 'Then we should all be happy, shouldn't we?'

They were glowering at each other when a heavy fist started banging on the door and Harvey's voice demanded he be let in.

Carl rose at once. 'The cavalry to the rescue,' he drawled mockingly, and went to unlock the door. 'It's all right,' he declared smoothly as Harvey, closely followed by Nina, brushed him aside. 'I haven't murdered her, though the provocation was great.'

'It looks as if you've had a damn good try,' Harvey growled ferociously, hunkering down before her. 'What the hell have you done to her?'

Eve smiled, grateful for his concern, then her eyes rose to meet Carl's. 'We argued, but I think we've reached an understanding now. I'm fine, really.'

Harvey growled, 'Well, you don't look it.'

Eve laughed hollowly. 'There was some pretty vicious close-hand stuff, but I survived.' Barely.

Carl leaned back casually against the doorpost and crossed his arms, viewing the scene before him cynically. 'You'll be pleased to know Eve has graciously decided to fulfil her contract.'

'It was a breathtaking performance, Eve,' Nina said honestly.

'I knew Colleen's girl had it in her,' Harvey added. 'When this is over, you must come and stay with me in Bel Air. Honey, you'll take Hollywood by storm.'

'A difficult thing to achieve from Max's bed,' Carl put in caustically. 'Your erstwhile protégée prefers to give private performances. Fortunately for me she's prepared to make an exception for this film. So let's not waste any more time on useless causes. We've already lost a week, thanks to her caprices, and we're going to have to re-shoot all her scenes. The sooner we get started, the sooner we finish. I'll give you half an hour to get yourself sorted out, then I'll expect you back downstairs.'

Harvey managed to find his voice to stop Carl in the doorway. 'Lord, man, you can't expect her to carry on after this!' he expostulated.

Carl shot her an arctic look. 'I can and she will. This is my film, Harvey, and if I want to work her right through the night, she'll damn well do it!' he stated coldly, and left.

The silence was uncomfortable.

'Evie, surely Carl was wrong?' Harvey proffered in confusion, standing up.

Eve rose too, setting her chin. 'No. I'm staying with Max,' she stated firmly. Crossing to the dressing-table, she looked in the mirror. The kohl had run, but, apart from her face being pale, there was no real sign of the storm that had barely passed.

'Here.' Nina offered her a tissue. 'I hope you know what you're doing, Eve. Max won't like it if he finds out.'

Their eyes met. Eve wondered just what the brunette knew. 'He won't find out,' she insisted firmly.

'I hope you're right,' Nina sighed. 'Come on, we'd better get you over to wardrobe.'

When she finally returned to the set, Eve was paler, but nothing else revealed the emotional turmoil going on inside her. Carl was in a foul mood, tongue dripping sarcasm from which nobody was immune. By the end of the day, everyone felt as if they had been put through a wringer. Eve bore the brunt of it. He could scarcely fault her acting, when each scene was put in the can with the minimum of takes, but his manner of directing her was laced with polite contempt.

She bore it in silence because she knew he had a right to be angry with her. Nobody liked to be made a fool of, especially in public, and she had done that for a week. Even so, it made her angry that everyone else was suffering too. He relented only when he had reduced Jenny to tears. He took her aside, and when they came back the young girl was smiling, though Carl looked grimmer than ever. When their eyes clashed, Eve knew he blamed her.

Before everyone disappeared they received a copy of the next day's script. Eve took hers without enthusiasm. The prospect of another day like today, followed by more of the same, was depressing.

'I trust you won't be too tired tonight to learn your lines?' Carl's acid voice made her jump, for she hadn't heard him approach. 'I'll expect you to be word-perfect in the morning,' he bit out harshly.

The small group of cast around her waited in silence for her reaction to that. They hadn't got over their resentment of her pretence, or the mood it had brought down on their innocent heads.

Stung, Eve flashed him a disdainful smile. 'Is that so?' Raising the script, she scanned it with a practised eye twice, then folded it neatly. She paced a few steps away, turned, looked him right in the eye, and proceeded to read off not just her lines, but everyone else's as well. 'I have a photographic memory,' she told her stunned audience at the end, but Carl in particular. 'I thought you ought to know just how much of a fool you've been taken for!' She stayed only long enough to see the jibe register, then turned and walked away.

She didn't feel proud, just sick and miserable. It had to be tiredness that made it virtually impossible to drum up her usual hatred and anger. That last trick had been merely spiteful, designed to hurt him the way he was constantly hurting her. Yet all it seemed to do was increase her unhappiness, and that was crazy. It seemed to say that Carl and happiness ought to go together.

Eve laughed at the ludicrous idea. Happiness would be never seeing him again.

CHAPTER SEVEN

IT WAS an uneasy group that sat around the breakfast table on the terrace the next morning. Eve hadn't seen Carl since their last vitriolic encounter the day before. She was feeling tense and depressed. What she had hoped for yesterday she had no real idea, but it hadn't happened. Everything was the same, except Carl. He was more coldly distant and angry than ever.

Nina had just made another abortive attempt at conversation when they heard the telephone ringing somewhere inside. Seconds later the housekeeper came out carrying an expensively wrapped package and a telephone. The former she laid on the table beside Eve's elbow.

'That was just delivered for you, miss, and Mr Nilsson is on the telephone,' she stated briskly, plugging in the extension and putting that by Eve too.

Silence fell as Eve stared at the package then reached for the telephone. She steeled herself and took a deep breath. 'Hello, Max,' she greeted evenly.

The line was so clear, he could have been standing next to her. 'Did my gift arrive?' he asked without preamble.

Her eyes returned to the package. 'Mrs Addison just brought me something. I—didn't know it was from you.'

'Good, good. If you haven't opened it, then do so now. I'll wait,' Max ordered smoothly.

Her heart starting to beat sickeningly, Eve lowered the receiver to the table and reluctantly reached for the parcel. Her eyes were drawn to the end of the table where Carl sat, watching with a mocking smile hovering about his lips. She didn't want to open it here, but Max wouldn't wait forever. Setting her lips, she tore away the

115

paper to reveal a heart-shaped box. When she flipped open the lid, nestling inside was a three-strand pearl necklace fastened with one diamond-encircled emerald.

A concerted gasp went round the table, and once again her eyes were drawn to Carl's. His contempt was withering. Going cold, she lifted the receiver to her ear, knowing what was expected of her.

'They're beautiful, Max, but I don't understand——' she intoned flatly.

'Happy birthday, my dear Eve. You see, I didn't forget,' Max congratulated with a low laugh.

He might not have forgotten, but she had. She was twenty-five today. Able, at last, to fulfil the agreement he said didn't exist. It was enough to make her forget her audience entirely. 'Is that all I'm going to get?'

'Now don't be greedy, my dear,' he advised silkily. 'Greedy girls can end up in prison.'

Eve went white, stiffening in her chair. 'I'm sorry,' she apologised thinly.

'It's not like you to be ungrateful, my dear,' he reproved her mildly.

She drew in a ragged breath. 'I am grateful, really.'

'I hope so, otherwise I might have to reconsider,' he mused.

Eve's free hand fluttered to her stomach. Oh, God, what had she done? 'Max, I've said I'm sorry. Please…please don't do anything hasty,' she said, shaken out of the calm that usually got her through their conversations.

'Are you doing as I asked?' Max questioned sharply.

'Yes, yes, I am.'

'And do you have anything to tell me?'

Oh, God! She had to say something to appease him. This time she had made too serious an error of judgement. Her eyes went to Carl's for the third time and locked there, making him sit up in sudden tension.

'He—er—he doesn't have any real evidence,' she said thickly, and flinched back from the violence in Carl's face.

'Good, very good, my dear. I must think of some way to reward you.'

Eve closed her eyes. 'You know there's only one reward I want,' she reminded him flatly.

'I know. Enjoy your birthday, my dear Eve. I'm proud of you.'

The connection was abruptly cut, and Eve lowered the receiver to the rest. She couldn't look at any of them, for she knew what they must be thinking. Reaching for the necklace, she closed the lid and pushed back her chair. 'Excuse me.'

Carl's hand came down on hers like a vice. 'Oh, no, you don't, you treacherous little cat. You don't throw me to the wolves and then get up and walk away!'

Eve had had just about as much as she could stand. She had just been humiliated by Max, she wouldn't take more from Carl. Shaking violently, she faced him, white and tense. 'Take your hands off me!' For a second or two she thought he was going to refuse, but then all at once she was free to stand up and glitter fiercely down at him, striking out defensively. 'What did I do that was such a surprise? You knew I'd do it, given the chance. You know I'd do it again, too. Well, I've kept my word to Max, and I'll keep it to you. I'll finish your precious little film, but in the name of God don't ever touch me again!'

'Gladly!' he shot back. 'I just hope your reward is worth it.'

She laughed. 'It will be. It might not last long, but while it does I'll know it was worth everything!' she finished passionately.

Carl's face was a stony mask. 'No doubt you'll be glad to know there won't be any work on my "precious little film" today. You can go away and gloat over your latest acquisition. My God, meeting you has been an education. I never knew I would find any woman quite so contemptible.'

'And I never knew I could grow to hate anyone quite so much as I do you. The end of this whole fiasco can't come soon enough!' she bit out harshly, and marched away, head held high.

But once out of sight she wiped ferociously at rapidly dampening cheeks. 'Oh, damn them! Damn them both!'

Eve spent the morning in her room. She made no excuse. She was hiding and didn't care who knew it. Just before lunch Nina knocked on the door.

'We're going in to Boston, do you want to come?' she invited, eyes scanning the other girl's pale cheeks.

'I don't think I'd be very good company, but thanks for asking. I appreciate it,' Eve declined with a faint smile.

Nina nodded. 'You'd be more than welcome, whatever the mood, but it's up to you. And listen, Eve, you know where my room is. Any time you want to talk, just knock.'

Those large brown eyes were uncomfortably keen. Eve smiled uneasily. 'I'll remember. Have a good time.'

As soon as she heard the cars leave, Eve went into her dressing-room and found her bikini and beach-robe. It was a lovely day out there, and now that she didn't have to avoid Carl she intended to enjoy it. What she was really doing, she knew, was trying to run away from her own sense of guilt. An impossible thing, but necessary to attempt.

The house was as silent as a tomb as she passed through it carrying a large towel and a bag with sun-glasses, cream and a book. On the beach, she spread the towel out near a large rock, slipped out of the robe, and settled down. The peace was soothing, the warmth gradually relaxing her into a comfortable doze. It was easy to imagine she was somewhere else, a place totally free of the pressures that hemmed her in. She slept.

It was the sudden raucous cry of startled gulls that eventually drew her back to consciousness. Sitting up groggily, she looked around, but could see neither the gulls nor the cause of their sudden panic. Stretching, she reached for the book and read for a while, but the soft crash of the waves was intrusive and magnetic. The water was blue and glittering and her overheated body craved the promised coolness.

Giving in to temptation, she rose gracefully to her feet and ran down into the water. It was colder than she'd expected and the shock of it clenched her muscles. But, having been brought up in England, she had weathered worse. Taking a deep breath, she dived into the next wave and struck out strongly.

Cramp caught her when she turned to come back. It tore through her leg, doubling her up in sudden and excruciating agony. She sank beneath the surface like a stone, hands clutching ineffectually at her stricken limb, then struggled to break surface for air. Worsening contractions made her moan.

She yelled for help, even though she knew it was hopeless, that everyone had gone. She was alone with her agony in an unforgiving sea. The instinct to survive made her bite her lip against the tearing pain and try to swim, but her strength had been sapped by the cramp and the cold water. With a sob, she felt herself slipping under again.

Then strong hands gripped her, lifting her face from the water so that she could gulp in the blessed air. Moaning, she tried to help by not struggling as her rescuer towed her rapidly back to the shore. Floundering in the shallows, she gasped through teeth clenched tight against the pain.

'Cramp.'

Firm hands found the spasmed muscle and began to massage. The cure was almost as bad as the affliction and she thrust her hand between her teeth, biting down hard. Gradually, though, the relief came, and she was able at length to open her eyes and look at her rescuer.

Dripping wet, his muscular torso glistening in the sunlight, it was Carl who bent over her. His concentration on her leg was total, and she was able to study him openly. It was a silly thing for such a momentous discovery, but she looked at where his long eyelashes were outlined in spiky relief against tanned cheeks, and thought: I love you.

Her lips parted in a soundless sigh. Her heart seemed to just swell up inside her chest, choking her throat, in a fierce moment of intense joy. She didn't hate him at all. She loved him. Had fallen in love with him on sight. She knew that with an absolute certainty. The hatred had been self-protection against the hurt. But it had been stripped away now, leaving the plain and simple truth. It was love. Totally.

She closed her eyes again as reality intruded. Loving Carl was hopeless. So hopeless that she moaned and shivered. At once the hands on her leg stopped work, and then one arm was under her back, the other under her knees, and he was lifting her, carrying her back up the beach to lay her on the sun-warmed towel.

Eve opened her eyes again and looked straight into deep blue ones, darkened now by concern.

'You little fool. Don't you know it's dangerous to go swimming alone? What were you trying to do, kill yourself?' he demanded fiercely, but Eve knew his anger came from fear at how close she had come to the latter.

'I didn't think,' she croaked.

His jaw flexed tensely as he dragged a hand over his hair. 'You never do!' he retorted furiously.

The realisation of her own feelings about him had made her too strung up to take his anger.

'Don't shout at me!' she cried, raising up on her elbow.

One hand pushed her down again and held her there. 'Shouting is the least of the things I feel like doing right

now. God give me strength! You could have drowned!'
he retorted, coming down beside her.

Tears of anger and futility turned her eyes to liquid
amethyst. 'Then you should have let me! I'd be out of
your hair once and for all. That's what you want, isn't
it?' she declared bitterly.

'What I want?' he ejaculated thickly, eyes lowering
from hers to the trembling fullness of her lips. Then he
swallowed and closed his eyes for an intense second.
When he looked at her again, blue eyes had darkened
to indigo. 'What I want, God help me, is you very much
alive and in my arms. Touching me the way I long to
touch you.'

Eve's breath lodged in her throat. Suddenly the air
between them was still and heavy, seething with that
never-to-be-forgotten excitement. She couldn't move,
could only watch as, with complete absorption, Carl followed the movement of his own hand from her shoulder,
between her breasts, over the flat stomach to the curve
of her hip. His touch burned, starting up flash-fires,
heating her blood—igniting the explosive awareness.

'Carl!' His name was a sighing moan on her lips.

It drew his eyes back to hers, and she was lost in them.
Gloriously lost.

'Touch me,' he commanded huskily, and her hands
fluttered to the taut, hair-roughened chest, fingers
running through the silky mat, drawing a gasp of
pleasure from him. He caught one hand, raising it to his
lips, tongue stroking a moist path over her palm.

Never had she imagined that such a small gesture could
be so erotic, but it was. Her body was suddenly flushed
with heat. Her eyes were mere slits as she watched him
draw one finger into his mouth, sucking it, tongue cir-
cling caressingly. She knew she ought to stop this now,
while she still could, but there were stronger forces at
work inside her. She loved him. She wanted to know,
just once, what it would feel like to be made love to by
him. She knew he didn't love her, accepted that, but he

did want her. Just this once, out of a lifetime. Surely that couldn't be wrong?

Her hand dropped back as he released her and began a tantalising voyage of discovery with lips and hands. His hand was a warm, possessive glide, smoothing away the scraps of her bikini and leaving her breathless. Lips and tongue followed. She didn't feel lusted after, but worshipped. She had never known love, didn't know what to expect. This gloriously sensual exploration was a mind-shattering revelation. She felt no shock at each intimate caress, only a growing wonder and delight— and a need to make him feel this too.

Not content to lie passive any longer, Eve reached for him and he subsided at once, abandoning himself to her. She explored him as he had her, glorying as he shuddered at the touch of her fingers and moaned at the brush of tongue and lips. He was naked too, she discovered, but it was impossible to be shy when his thickly uttered words of encouragement urged her on to boldness.

Desire mounted, breaking through the bonds of their restraint, and Carl took control once more with a groan, moving over her, caresses growing more and more wild and urgent. Long kisses dazzled the senses, driving them on with a reckless abandon, to a shivering, moaning entanglement of golden limbs and glistening bodies.

The fire they had stoked so carefully became a raging conflagration. Eve arched into his body as Carl parted her thighs with his. She cried out when he came into her strongly, but not from pain, although it was there fleetingly. No, from a wonderment at the feeling of oneness with him. Of knowing that this of all men was hers, now and forever, no matter what happened.

Then Carl was moving within her, building the spiralling coil of tension to a pitch where she thought she couldn't possibly go on without shattering. Pleasure exploded around her and she cried out, hands holding Carl close as he shuddered against her. She floated, heart pounding joyously. Fulfilment brought tears to her eyes.

Nothing that happened to her would ever match the beauty of what they had just shared, and her heart swelled with love.

So she was all the more shocked when Carl rolled away from her and sat up, arms crossed on his knees, forehead resting on them. Concerned, she came up on her elbow, but as she did so Carl rose, stalking down to the water and plunging in. Bewildered and hurt, she sat up, staring at his flashing arms as he began a distance-eating crawl. After a minute he turned and came back, wading out of the water to where his jeans lay discarded. Heedless of his wet body, he pulled them on and strode back to her.

He came to a halt above her, hands on hips. When he bent, suddenly, she flinched, but he only reached for her robe and tossed it to her.

'Put that on,' he commanded brusquely.

Suddenly embarrassed, Eve couldn't draw it over her cooling flesh quickly enough. Once she was covered, Carl dropped to his knees before her, hands doubled into fists on his thighs.

'Right,' he said shortly. 'Start explaining.'

'What?' Eve gasped, totally confused. Minutes ago they had been making love, and now he was like a stranger.

'At this precise moment I'm having trouble keeping my hands off you, so open those sexy lips and start talking!'

She swallowed. 'About what?'

'About how Max's mistress turns out to have been a virgin,' he grated through tightly clenched teeth.

Heat scorched into her cheeks. 'Oh.'

'Yes, oh,' Carl mimicked angrily. 'I'm listening. This had better be good.'

Eve took a giant mental step back into safety, trying to retrieve a situation suddenly fraught with danger. 'I have nothing to say,' she stated flatly, and hard hands bit into her shoulders, jerking her up to her knees.

'Wrong, darling. You have one hell of a lot to say. I want to know what's going on, and I want to know now!' he growled, shaking her.

Her hands went to his arms for balance. 'Nothing is going on,' she replied huskily.

'Don't take me for a fool. Max has been at some pains to tell the world you're his mistress, and you've been backing him up. What game are you playing?' Carl's eyes narrowed as he witnessed the alarm in her eyes. 'Are you in some sort of trouble?'

Eve realised now just how foolish it had been to give in to her need. Now Carl was demanding to know things she just couldn't tell him, because it went beyond Max to her mother, and that was sacrosanct.

She tried to laugh, but it was a poor effort. 'Don't be silly. What trouble could I be in?'

'You tell me,' he ground out bluntly.

Her heart gave a sickening lurch as she realised she was making a mess of it. She must pull herself together, and fast, if she wanted him to believe her. Taking a deep breath, she met his eyes. 'I'm not in trouble,' she asserted levelly.

His eyes bored into hers relentlessly. 'If that's so, why the pretence?'

He was like a dog with a bone, and she cast about wildly for an answer. 'Max asked me to,' she finally offered.

For an instant Carl frowned, then his brows lifted. 'I see,' he said slowly, and let her go. 'Max asked you, and you agreed, just like that?' he continued smoothly.

Her nerves jolted. Now what? 'Yes.'

'Why?' The one-word question was silky and deadly.

Eve stared, heart knocking painfully in her chest. 'Why?'

Carl nodded, folding his arms across his chest, giving the impression of being willing to wait forever for her reply. 'That's what I said. Why did you agree?'

One hand fluttered to her temple, as if that could help her think up a believable reason in the next ten seconds. Something did, for suddenly she had an answer. 'Because he promised me all the money, jewellery and designer clothes I could possibly want,' she declared defiantly, certain that would put him off as it had in the past.

'I see,' Carl said again, and the way he said it made Eve think that he really did see, and that was unnerving. 'So that's what you want out of life, is it?' he asked next, in a milder tone.

Primal instinct told her to beware, but she was committed now and had to go on. 'Yes,' she confirmed uneasily.

For long drawn-out seconds Carl studied her, until she wanted to scream. Sensing it, he asked, 'That's the truth?'

The limb she was on shook. 'It is,' she agreed, watching him like a transfixed rabbit. His anger had gone, evaporating like mist in sunlight. He was totally relaxed and growing more assured by the second.

He smiled. 'You can change your mind if you want to,' he offered her the choice, making her nerves jangle in alarm.

'Why should I want to?' she asked warily, heart sinking as she realised she was facing a Carl she hadn't met before. She was way out of her depth.

The smile broadened. 'Because if it is true, then I'm putting in my bid. I can offer all that Max can, plus great sex and a chance of movie stardom. If it is true, then the woman you make yourself out to be will take the offer. Leap at it, in fact. Of course, if it isn't, all you have to do is tell me the real truth.'

Eve heard the trap close over her with a deafening crash. She stared at him, pale as a ghost, knowing she had brought it all on herself. 'You devil!'

'And you're a fraud, Eve Hunter.' There was triumph in his blue eyes as he scanned her face. 'Want to try again?' he said gently.

'Go to hell!' she shot back gruffly.

He reached out a hand and trailed a finger down her cheek. 'I've been there. I can show you the way out, but you'll have to tell me the truth. Think about it.'

She set her chin. 'You're talking in riddles. I've already told you the truth.'

Impatience and something else flickered across his face, and then was gone. 'I'll give you time to change your mind, but it's only fair to warn you, I haven't given up. In the meantime, I'm going to get to know you, Eve Hunter. The real you, that is. Oh, not here. We need somewhere neutral—just you and me. I know a restaurant down the coast that I think you'll appreciate. We'll go there for dinner tonight, and if you don't want to talk, we can always dance. Seven-thirty in the hall, and remember, I'm not Max. I don't need to have all men drooling over you. Wear something a little more you.'

'And if I don't choose to go?' she challenged, with all the calmness she could manage in the face of this disaster.

One eyebrow rose. 'You can refuse if you want to, but then I'd have to start wondering what you have to hide,' he returned smoothly.

He was beating her at every turn. Now she would have to go. 'Why are you doing this?' she demanded huskily.

'Why did you let me make love to you?' he countered.

Eve's lips twisted bitterly. 'It seemed a good idea at the time, but now I can't regret it enough!' she snapped back.

Carl rose nimbly to his feet with a low laugh. 'Do you? I find myself not regretting it at all.'

She drew in a sharp, disbelieving breath at that goad. 'I think I hate you!' she cried, eyes troubled and defensive.

'Hate away, but you might give some thought to trusting me instead,' he advised abruptly, then turned, collected his clothes from where they had fallen in his rush to rescue her earlier, and disappeared into the trees.

Eve stared after him. Suddenly she was very much afraid of him. His mind was like a steel trap. Her reckless impulse to make love with him had revealed one piece of a jigsaw puzzle and now he wasn't going to let up until he had each piece and had fitted them together. That was what scared her. He didn't need much help. Now that he knew things weren't what they seemed he wouldn't take as gospel anything he heard and saw. He had implied he would know the truth when he heard it, and his offer told her he hadn't heard it yet.

But her determination was just as strong as his. She could not, and would not, tell him just because he had uncovered a mystery and wanted to know the truth. That wasn't a good enough reason for breaking her promise to her mother, for that was what Carl would want to know if she ever revealed just how Max was black-mailing her.

So she must go with him tonight and bluff her way out. She must, if possible, put behind her what had happened this afternoon. Forget that she loved him, because he was dangerous and she couldn't afford to be vulnerable to her own awakened emotions.

Slowly she collected together her belongings and walked back up to the house to shower and change. She spent the rest of the afternoon in her room, not wishing to come into contact with Carl again until she was fully prepared. Tonight was going to be far from easy.

She thought of defying his advice on what to wear, but she hated the clothes Max preferred and longed to feel more herself. So she chose a simple white two-piece and left her hair loose about her face. Make-up she kept to a minimum, and added only a simple pair of diamond studs for her ears and a wristwatch. Slipping her feet into white court shoes, she was ready.

When she descended the stairs, Carl was already waiting. Tonight he wore a simple black dinner-suit, pristine white silk shirt and black bow-tie. He looked up as he heard her, and that elemental spark was in the air, confusing and exciting by turns.

'Now that,' he declared warmly, 'I like.'

It struck her at once, the change in him. He was turning on the charm, and her trouble was that every sense she possessed was responding to it.

Her acidly issued, 'I'm so pleased,' was designed not only as a put-down, but also to calm her own rioting nerves.

Carl's response was merely to grin and usher her out. He had brought his car up to the house, and he helped her into her seat before climbing in the other side. His nearness made the confined space inside the sporty car even more claustrophobic. She could feel his confidence and it acted on her nerves, making her wish she had refused after all, but she was committed, and all she could do was carry on gamely.

Once they were out on the highway, she cleared her throat. 'Where exactly are we going?' she asked, glancing his way, and saw his lips curve as he smiled.

'It's a surprise,' he drawled, without taking his eyes off the road.

Her heart fluttered at his attractive profile, and she warned herself sharply that he was now extremely dangerous. He was using his charm on her deliberately, and she was all too susceptible to it. The only answer was to keep him at a distance. 'I hate surprises,' she returned icily.

Carl laughed. 'Really? That I find hard to believe when you throw out so many of your own.'

'That's not true!' she retorted, drawn despite her resolve.

'You should change places with me, darling. But I'm on to you now. I feel like shouting "Will the real Eve Hunter please stand up"!' he countered mockingly.

Eve drew in her breath. '*If* there is another me, why should she reveal herself?' she challenged.

'Because she needs help,' he returned steadily, and flicked her a glance.

That was the sort of remark that set her heart thudding in its accuracy. 'You're in the right profession with an imagination like yours,' she retorted acidly.

'Then shall I drive to the nearest motel, book a room and we'll go straight to bed?' Carl enquired dulcetly.

She stifled an angry gasp, realising her tongue had led her on to shaky ground again. 'You promised me dinner,' she reminded him shortly, attempting a recovery. 'Don't try weaselling out of it.'

Carl laughed, a low, husky, sexy sound. 'If anyone's weaselling, it's you, darling. But don't worry, this time I intend to satisfy my appetites in the right order.'

Eve didn't find that comforting, nor the fact that his bald promise set her pulse throbbing crazily. She wished he would stop calling her darling, too. It was doing strange things to her spine. Setting her lips, she gave up the unequal battle of wits with him and kept silent for the rest of the journey.

Carl's chosen restaurant was on a secluded stretch of coastline, yet, for all its isolation, the car park was full. They managed to find a spot, and he helped her out, keeping his hand under her elbow as he ushered her inside. There was a band playing in the large dining-room and couples were already dancing there, but they were shown to a table on the terrace lit only by coloured lights on the trellis and a small candle-lamp on the table.

The whole atmosphere was soothing, with the promise of good food. Added to the balmy evening air, it was also undoubtedly romantic. How right he was that it would appeal to her, and how unnerving the admission. It told her that he saw her far more clearly now than he had ever done.

As she sat down, Eve was aware that they were being watched by several pairs of eyes, and it occurred to her, rather belatedly, that she could be recognised.

'Relax,' Carl directed her once he had ordered cocktails for them both, showing her just how easily he was reading her mind. 'This isn't Max's sort of place, nor is it likely that anyone who did recognise you would bother to tell him. He doesn't have friends, and nobody wants to be his enemy. If you want to be wary of anyone, it's that female barracuda Mrs Addison.'

'The housekeeper?' Eve exclaimed in surprise, diverted.

Their drinks arrived, and Carl waited until they were alone again before answering. 'Believe it or not, she once had the dubious pleasure of occupying your position. She didn't have pride enough to leave when she was superseded, but she's spiteful enough to carry tales. What do you want to eat?'

Eve barely heard the question, though she accepted the menu. Mrs Addison? Yet why not? As a younger woman she would have been attractive—before bitterness destroyed it. She shivered, and concentrated on the food, deciding on avocado with prawns and a fillet of sole. Carl placed the order, approving her choice by having the same.

Then he sat back, crossing his long legs and regarding her sardonically. 'So, tell me all about Eve.'

Despite all her earlier warnings not to let him disarm her, her lips twitched and she couldn't resist it. 'Should I fasten my seat-belt? Is it going to be a bumpy night?'

Carl stared at her, arrested for a moment by the way her face had lit up, then he laughed appreciatively. 'Ah, a film buff.'

Half smiling, Eve twirled her glass. 'I was weaned on them,' she admitted.

'Did you have a strange childhood? Your mother was a household name.'

'True, but I didn't know who she was. She left when I was tiny. In this day and age, can having only one parent be said to be strange?'

'More the norm, I would say. Which makes it odd that you realised how deep your parents' relationship was if your mother wasn't there.'

'Not really. Oh, I resented her for a long time,' Eve admitted, frowning a little. 'For Dad's sake, actually. Then years later, when I saw her again, I realised he hadn't needed it.' Her face revealed the amazement she'd felt at the time, and she leant forward, eyes shining. 'You only had to see them! Carl, it was like—coming home. You could go anywhere, for any length of time, and yet only one place is home. They were that for each other. Then I knew that the absence had hurt Mum, too. But they were wise enough to keep what they had by letting go of a little.'

'You didn't feel left out?' Carl put in softly.

Eve shook her head. 'No, never. I always knew I was loved too. But it's not the same sort of love as between a man and a woman,' she qualified, and vivid memories of her own feelings for this man who sat mere inches away made it impossible to go on. She was glad of the interruption caused by the arrival of their food, which ended all talk until they were alone again.

'He must miss her,' Carl observed then, and when she looked at him in surprise, her thoughts far away, he prompted, 'Your father.'

'Yes,' she agreed uncomfortably.

'What did he do? He wasn't an actor?'

'No. He was a farmer,' she revealed with a fond laugh. 'They sound a very odd couple. But she needed his gentleness and he needed her vitality. Farming was his life, he hated giving it up.'

'Then why did he? Or was it financial?' Carl urged her on with casual interest.

'He needed the money for——' Suddenly she was brought up short, aware that she was within an ace of revealing everything. My God, he had her bewitched! Abruptly she sat back, eyeing him warily.

'For?' Carl prompted.

Breathing deeply, she smiled and shrugged. 'Something else. Anyway, it was all too sad. I'd prefer not to talk about it.'

Not by a flicker did Carl reveal if he was frustrated or not. 'As you wish. What about you? What did you do before Max came into your life?' he said, obligingly changing tack.

That was like stepping from the frying-pan into the fire, but she couldn't avoid it, for that would be too obvious. 'I worked for his London company,' she declared, holding his gaze levelly, defying him to make what he would of it.

'Ah.'

Her eyes narrowed. 'What does that mean?' she asked suspiciously.

He shrugged. 'Just—ah. So you worked for Max. In what capacity?'

He had the unhappy knack of asking questions she would rather not answer. Eve debated saying nothing, but knew he could very easily find out for himself anyway. 'I arranged loans,' she told him shortly, but couldn't allow him to start his brain working on that. She rushed on, 'And while we're at it, I might as well give you the complete run-down. I grew up on a farm until I was old enough to go to boarding-school. There I did moderately well at most subjects. I was fortunate enough to get a job straight from college. I was never short of boyfriends, but no lovers. End of story.'

Carl reached for his glass and took an appreciative mouthful of wine, savouring it before finally saying, 'Why so defensive?'

Her teeth snapped together because she had made another mistake. 'You make me defensive. I haven't asked you intimate questions about your life and family.'

He tipped his head. 'Was I getting too close?' he asked mildly, and held up a hand as she stiffened. 'You needn't answer that. As for my life, you know a lot of it already, but ask away, I've nothing to hide.'

'Meaning that I have?' she returned, smarting.

'Well, have you?' he queried softly.

Chest heaving a little, she took a steadying breath. 'Are your parents still living?' she asked abruptly.

Carl grinned. 'They are. They're retired now, and run a stable in Connecticut. I have a brother who's a navy flyer, and a sister who married an Australian sheep-farmer. I have an apartment in LA, down the coast, and another in Manhattan, but my favourite home is a house not far from my parents. Anything else you'd like to know?'

My God, he was galling! 'Are you married?' she asked sweetly.

He wasn't put out at all. 'Not any more. My wife and I parted amicably about thirteen years ago. Since then I've had girlfriends, and one or two who lived with me for a time, but no one special,' he informed her easily.

He was toying with her, damn him! She felt angry and frustrated. 'Now what do we talk about for the rest of the evening?' she asked acidly.

Carl's eyes glittered. 'Oh, we'll think of something.'

Eve swallowed as her nerves responded immediately. 'Oh, this is ridiculous. I don't know why I'm sitting here with you!' she declared, pushing her empty plate away, more than a little surprised that she had been able to eat at all.

'Yes, you do,' he argued softly.

'I don't!' she declared firmly.

'Suit yourself,' he shrugged at once, and held out his hand. 'Come and dance.'

She didn't want to go, but he didn't allow her to refuse, pulling her stiff body with him. Only once before had she danced with him. As she went into his arms on the dance-floor she wondered if he remembered. It was as if it had been years ago, so much had happened. But one thing hadn't changed: the magic was still there. It was foolish, but she couldn't resist him. All her rigidity melted away. Her head went to his shoulder, eyes closing, and one hand stole up, allowing her hand to curve around his neck, fingers trailing in his hair.

How long they danced she didn't know, and when Carl finally drew away her eyes rose and locked with his bemusedly.

'Let's go.' Carl's voice was gruff, and there was no fight in her as she let him guide her back to their table to collect her bag.

On the long drive back, Carl tuned the radio to a station playing soft music. The warmth and the muffled growl of the engine combined with the music to send her to sleep. She awoke to motionless silence, and the brush of warm lips on hers. Instinct had her lips parting to the insistence of his tongue, and with a sigh of satisfaction she turned into the arms that reached for her, and the kiss deepened.

It was a sweet ache, the need and longing and love. Each kiss seemed to draw her soul from her. His hand slipped beneath her top, gliding over satin skin until it reached her breast, pushing the lacy bra aside to caress the ultra-sensitive peak.

Eve was lost instantly, drowning in the pleasure that only he could give her. She moaned when his lips left hers to plunder her neck, sending shivers down her spine.

'Eve.' Her name was a breath of sound in her ear.

'Yes?' She didn't want to talk, she just wanted this to go on and on forever.

'Tell me the truth,' he sighed, tongue tracing the shell-like convolutions of her ear.

Eve froze, hardly able to believe her ears. She struggled away, eyes searching his in the pale light which was coming, she vaguely registered, from the front of the house. The annoyance on his face told her she hadn't imagined it.

'Oh, God!' That was a mean, underhand... 'Let me go!' she ordered bitterly. 'You miscalculated. You're not that irresistible!' she snarled, feeling sick and angry at how easily he had worked his charms. A little longer and she might even have told him!

Carl didn't try to stop her as she scrambled from the car, but he was out of his door and by her side in a flash, cutting off her escape.

Eve backed away, lips trembling. 'You'll try any trick, won't you?' she charged thickly.

The only sign of his anger at losing was the glitter in his eyes. 'I'm determined to find out the truth, Eve, any way I have to.'

'You're despicable!'

'Tell me and I'll stop right now,' he declared stonily.

'Never! Do your worst, I'll tell you nothing!' she cried, and thrust him aside, running into the house.

Carl stared after her. 'Remember you said that, darling,' he said softly, 'because I'm prepared to stop at nothing.'

CHAPTER EIGHT

EVE discovered just how determined Carl was to drag the truth from her over the next few days. He didn't make the same mistake of trying to seduce her, but changed tack completely. Suddenly she could do nothing right. However well a scene went, Carl found something wrong with her performance. The first few times it happened, she thought she was over-reacting, that she had, in fact, done something wrong. But as time went by and almost every scene was shot over and over, she realised it was deliberate.

When she taxed him with it, he didn't deny it, just crossed his arms and regarded her from beneath raised brows.

'I'm directing the film; if I say it isn't right, we'll keep on doing a scene until I'm satisfied.'

Eve ground her teeth impotently. 'But you're wasting time. I told you we had to get the filming done before Max gets back,' she argued. The constant delay was a mounting worry now.

'I know you told me, but I don't know why,' Carl returned unperturbed.

'Because he mustn't know I'm helping you. He wouldn't like it,' she repeated in frustration.

A finger under her chin tipped her eyes to meet his. 'Words, Eve. You're remarkably talented at stringing them together, but are they the truth? Be fair. You've lied so often, how can I tell? However, I'm sure that if you tried you could come up with something to convince me.'

Violet eyes darkened angrily. 'Why can't you just leave well enough alone?'

Exasperation got the better of him for an instant. 'Because it's far from well enough, you little fool!'

'Oh, mind your own business!' she cried in angry desperation and retreated from the fray, leaving Carl grim-faced behind her.

The rest of the cast and crew watched mystified as this battle of wills developed around them. Initial amusement soon gave way to frustration and anger, though. The word 'cut' was anticipated with mounting disgust, for it generally heralded yet another take.

After a week of it, the seeds of rebellion among the cast were finding fertile ground.

'I don't know what's between you two,' Dick growled out one afternoon as they prepared to retake a scene, 'and I don't want to know. I'm just fed up with paying for it too. Get it sorted out, honey, or I, for one, am quitting!'

At the end of the scene, when Carl once again called for another take, Eve intercepted Dick's fulminating glare and decided she just had to try and do something. Clenching her fists at her sides, she walked purposefully to where Carl sat talking to his assistant. He glanced up as she halted, eyebrows raised in mild enquiry.

'Don't you think this is all rather ridiculous?' she challenged. 'There was nothing wrong with that take and you know it. What is it going to take to make you stop?'

Carl dismissed his assistant with a look before answering, 'You know the answer as well as I do. One of these days you're going to have to decide who and what you are. The sooner you do, the sooner this will stop.'

She stared at him helplessly. 'Why are you doing this? Do you hate me so much?'

His face closed up. 'For once I'm trying to keep my feelings for you out of the way. A cool head is what's needed here,' he returned levelly.

'But all you're doing is compromising the film!' she pointed out despairingly.

'Priorities change. We have to be adaptable,' Carl re-joined smoothly.

Eve pressed angry lips together. 'And now your priority is to mess up my life.'

He smiled coolly. 'That's one way of looking at it. Now, unless you have something to say, you're just wasting my time. We have another take to do. Perhaps you can get it right this time.'

Eve spun away before she gave in to the temptation to wipe that look from his face. Hell could freeze over before she gave in.

A few days later Nina dropped down beside Eve on the couch. Dinner was over and the others had all dispersed on errands of their own.

'Well,' Nina sighed expressively, crossing her slim legs, 'it's been an interesting ten days, all told. When do the rest of us get to know what's going on?'

'Ask Carl,' Eve suggested shortly.

'Funny, he told me to ask you,' the brunette responded drily.

Glancing around, Eve encountered that disconcertingly penetrating brown gaze, and closed her magazine with a sigh. 'All I'm prepared to say is that Carl wants to know something that's none of his business. He chose to involve you all, not me.'

'Something happened, didn't it?' Nina returned cautiously. 'The day we went to Boston? When we left you two were at daggers drawn. When we returned, the rules had changed.'

Eve glanced down at her hands. 'Nina——'

The brunette laughed wryly. 'Oh, it's all right. I'm not going to pry. A simple yes or no will do.'

Eve sighed heavily. 'Yes.'

Nina touched her arm sympathetically. 'I'll guess at the rest. Just remember, in lieu of family, you can always talk to me,' she said, before picking up another magazine from the coffee-table.

The mention of family reminded Eve that she hadn't telephoned her father for some time. He knew she was in America, though not where or why, and because of the time difference he left calling to her. She did a rapid calculation and decided that if she left it until around midnight her father should just be getting up at the Swiss clinic her mother was in.

The house had been silent for a long time when Eve made her way to the library to make her call. She always telephoned from there because, being situated at the back of the house and rarely used, it offered the least chance of detection. Switching on the desk-lamp, she sat down and dialled direct. The delay was minimal before she heard Gerald Hunter's voice at the other end of the line.

'Hello, Dad, did I wake you?' she greeted huskily, her throat closing over with emotion.

'Eve? It's wonderful to hear your voice, love. No, you didn't wake me. I don't tend to sleep much these days,' he enlarged with a revealing sigh.

Eve rested her elbow on the desk and dropped her head into her hand. 'How are you?'

'Oh, I'm fine, fine,' he returned, with determined cheerfulness.

Her voice lowered. 'And Mum? How's she?'

There was silence then, for a second, before her father admitted sadly, 'She's fading, Eve, right before my eyes. It won't be long now, I think.'

'Oh, Dad, I'm so sorry!' Tears overflowed, tracking silently down her cheeks. 'I wish I could be there with you.'

'What could you do, love?' he responded sensibly. 'She wouldn't know you. She doesn't know me. Besides, she'd want you to remember her the way she was. I love her, Eve, but I want her to go. She isn't my Colleen any more. She left a long time ago. All I want is to see her at peace at last. So don't be sorry, love.'

Eve swallowed, her throat aching. 'All right, I'll try. Tell Mum I love her, Dad. I love you, too.' Her throat closed over completely, and it was a second or two before she could go on. 'How is everything else? Do you have enough money?'

'More than enough, love, now. I think I'll be in touch before you this time, Eve,' Gerald added gently.

Eve caught her breath. 'I understand. Let me know as soon as it's over?'

'I will, love. Now I'd better let you get to bed, you've a working day ahead of you. Take care of yourself, Eve.'

'You too, Dad. Goodbye.'

She replaced the receiver carefully, overwhelmed by sadness. She knew her father was right, the end would be a blessing, yet the tears came anyway. In the quiet room, she allowed all the misery and grief to pour out.

Strong hands on her shoulders barely registered, nor her name as a low voice groaned, 'Eve.' Yet she obeyed their command to rise and be turned into a warm chest, arms closing safely round her. The comfort was immense. All the security she ever needed was right there. Slowly the tears stopped falling, and dried on her cheeks, but she stayed where she was, savouring the moment.

'So, Colleen MacManus isn't dead,' Carl declared gently. 'That's what this is all about, isn't it, Eve?'

She froze, eyes shooting open in alarm. The arms that held her were now more of a threat than comfort, and she pushed herself away hurriedly to blink up at him.

'You heard?' Horror swiftly turned to anger. 'How dare you listen in to a private conversation?'

Carl slowly lowered his arms, hands slipping into trouser pockets. 'It wasn't intentional. I came in here to do some thinking and fell asleep. Your voice woke me. You can imagine my surprise when the first words I heard were to give your mother your love.'

He hadn't heard it all! Relief lent wings to her powers of invention. 'And so you assumed I was talking about Colleen MacManus. It wouldn't occur to you that my father married again.'

Blue eyes narrowed suspiciously. 'That has the un-mistakable ring of desperation about it. You're lying, but why?'

Eve's mouth went dry. 'You have absolutely no right to call me a liar!' she croaked.

'Don't I?' he queried softly. 'You've reached new heights of mendacity. There's nothing straightforward about any of this. You're a mistress, but you aren't. Your mother's dead, but she isn't.'

Her lips parted on anxious breathing. 'I've told you that's just not true.'

Carl reached out and traced the line of her lips with a gentle finger. 'There's something you ought to know about me, darling,' he declared in a low, measured tone.

Heart jolting, she swallowed. 'What?'

He half smiled. 'I find enigmas intriguing. I have to get to the bottom of them. Something has you running scared, and I want to know what it is. I mean to know. You're not the sort that frightens easily—not on your own behalf.'

Eve forced an incredulous laugh through a tight throat. 'I've never heard such a load of——' His fingers increasing their pressure cut off her jeering words.

'Don't waste your breath on more lies. Save it for the truth. You'll tell me in the end.'

A growing sense of losing all control of the situation roused her dormant anger again. 'There's nothing to tell,' she insisted firmly.

Carl released her, shrugging. 'Suit yourself, but time is on my side. Max can't be away much longer, can he?'

Paling, she stiffened. 'Is that a threat?' she demanded, and missed the slight narrowing of his eyes.

'Perhaps,' was all he said.

By her sides, her hands balled into impotent fists. He knew how desperately she wanted the filming to finish before Max returned! Now, out of sheer curiosity, he was jeopardising everything. It wasn't even as if he really cared! He just couldn't bear the idea of being taken for a ride. He was going to pay her back for all the cheating and lies, and he didn't care who got hurt in the process.

She lifted her chin defiantly. 'You don't frighten me.'

Reluctant admiration softened his face for an instant, then was gone. 'No, but something does, and that's what I intend to find out,' he stated firmly, and, after waiting for a reaction that she withheld, he turned and crossed to the door, pausing only long enough to look back and say, 'Think about it. Think very hard. Goodnight, Eve.' The door clicked softly shut behind him.

Eve sank down weakly on to the seat behind her, not knowing what to do. She hated him for trying to manipulate her in this way. Even if it were her secret to tell, she wouldn't, not now. However, she couldn't afford to ignore his threats. There was just too much at stake. She had to find a way to foil him. To stop him following a path that was simply too dangerous to those she loved. But what?

It came to her the next day, the answer so obvious that she was amazed she hadn't thought of it during that long, sleepless night. After another frustrating day of retakes, when she was so very much aware of Carl's eyes following her every move, on or off set, she felt like screaming. Dinner was more of the same, and she could barely eat a thing. She was glad when Carl took himself off to consult with his technicians, leaving her to find what relaxation she could. She went to her room early, right after Max's call, but not to bed. Standing under the needle-sharp spray of the shower, willing the water to ease away her tension, Eve saw the road she must take very clearly.

Shivering a little, she turned off the water, reaching for a large fluffy towel and wrapping herself in its warmth. Carl had given her the answer. He had told her that she had two choices—tell the truth, or, if she insisted she had, then take his offer. Well, she couldn't tell him the secret, but she could make him believe the lie. She was Colleen MacManus's daughter, wasn't she?

Feeling even colder, Eve padded into her bedroom and sank down on to the edge of the bed. Biting her lip, she stared down at the palms of her hands. There were harsh facts to be faced. Verbal agreement of Carl's offer would only be the beginning. She would be agreeing to becoming his lover. She would have to sleep with him.

Strange how the thought of doing that so coldbloodedly could induce pain, when she had been prepared to do the same with Max so unemotionally. But that was because she hadn't loved Max. She would have shut him out of the heart of her. It wasn't possible with Carl. Against him, her defences were puny and weak. What she contemplated cheapened her feelings for him, even if he wouldn't know it. That would hurt her, for she would be destroying perhaps her only chance of gaining his respect.

Sighing with lonely resignation, she traced the tiny scars where her nails had punctured her palm that first day. Why was she hesitating? It had always been doomed. From the very beginning, fate had been against her. Loving Carl was hopeless anyway. She wouldn't be relinquishing anything that had ever been hers. Besides, surely her mother's last days were worth any pain? She couldn't start to be selfish now.

That was the deciding factor that brought Eve to her feet, and sent her into her dressing-room to search out her sexiest nightdress. Made of ivory silk and lace, it clung lovingly to the contours of her body. Slit to the thigh, it gave enticing glimpses of flesh at every step, and the lace cups of the bodice barely covered her breasts. There was a négligé to match, and she slipped it on before padding back into the bedroom to brush her hair into a platinum halo about her face, and dab Poison on to every pulse-spot.

A glance in the cheval-mirror showed her a longlegged, sexy woman, with glittering violet eyes. There was seduction in every line, every pore. Eve shuddered once, took a deep breath and slipped into character. She had never thought she would be grateful to Velda Maxwell, but tonight she needed her.

The house was silent as she switched off the light and stepped into the corridor. It occurred to her that she didn't even know if Carl was in his room. He had gone out soon after dinner and she hadn't heard him return. Yet he must have, for there was a faint glow shining under his door as she approached it. Before she could change her mind, she knocked once, softly, and went in.

Carl was in bed. That was the first and only thing she saw as she leant back against the closed door. Torso bare, he lay propped against the headboard, reading. The book had been lowered at her knock, and now he slowly closed it, regarding her silk-clad figure with an intense stillness.

The silence that seethed across the room was intimidating. Eve knew, with a fast-beating heart, that if she didn't do something quickly to break it, her nerve would go. But her mouth was like a desert in the face of Carl's silently waiting person.

'I came to ask you something,' she began, her voice low and husky—and unintentionally sexy.

For a second Carl remained still, then he twisted to place the book on the bedside table before crossing his arms. 'Well?'

The tip of her tongue appeared to moisten her lips, and her nerves jolted as his eyes dropped to her mouth, remaining locked there as if in helpless fascination. 'I...wanted to know if the offer you made was still open, because if it is I'd like to take you up on it.'

In the bed, Carl stiffened. 'Offer?'

Taking her courage, Eve pushed herself away from the door and approached the bed. Fingers trailing on the covers, she glanced up at him from beneath her lashes. 'Yes. You remember. You told me to think, and I have. Why should I stay with Max when you have so much more to offer?' As the last word left her lips her heart quailed, for she could have sworn that what she saw reflected in Carl's eyes was an explosive anger. Yet a second later there was nothing to be seen. No sign at all as to how he received the news, and she decided she must have imagined it in the low lighting.

She wasn't prepared for the intense disappointment she experienced when his teeth flashed in a devilish grin and his hand moved to sweep back the covers beside him. 'In that case, sweetheart, why don't you come and join me?' he suggested smoothly, eyes locking with hers.

Now was not the time to have doubts, so she met that look squarely as she moved round the bed. Allowing the négligé to slip from her shoulders, she climbed in beside him. In one smooth movement Carl drew the covers over her, and at the same time his powerful frame loomed over her, trapping her against the pillows.

Blue eyes roved the pale oval of her face. 'So,' he muttered huskily, 'you've decided to stop playing games, have you? At last I'm seeing the real Eve Hunter?'

'You said you wanted to, and there's no need to pretend if the truth will get me what I want,' she returned in a dry little voice.

Beneath the covers, his fingers found her shoulder and traced a line down her arm. 'And what do you want?' he probed, catching her fluttering hand in his, bringing it up to his lips.

Her throat closed over on the one husky word. 'You.'

'Ah,' he breathed softly, lips burning her palm. 'Your hands are cold. Are you nervous, Eve? Surely not of me?'

Heart pounding in agitation, Eve was still aware beneath it all of that elemental *frisson* that his touch induced. 'I...was afraid you might have changed your mind.'

Carl laughed deep in his throat. 'And that would upset all your plans, wouldn't it?'

In the recesses of her mind, unease set up an alarm. Was there more behind his words than there appeared? She couldn't allow him to start questioning her decision.

Sensing danger, she went on the attack. Forcing her tense body to relax, she raised her free hand to his chest, running her fingers through the silky mat of hair there.

'Oh, Carl, let's not talk.' She pouted sensually. 'That's not what I came here for.'

Beneath lowered lids, his eyes glittered brilliantly. 'Oh, honey, believe me, I know it,' he declared tautly. 'Tell me what you want me to do, Eve. Show me.'

Eve spoke the words that took her beyond the point of recall, unaware of the desperation she revealed. 'Kiss me. Make love to me until I can't think at all!' she commanded, and, freeing her other hand, used both to pull him down to her.

Recklessly she used lips and hands, willing him to drive all power of thought from her, so that for as long as it lasted she need not remember why she was doing this. A frantic sob caught at her throat as Carl returned her kisses and caresses. Yet the oblivion she sought didn't come, and, despairing, her attempts to find it drove her on to wildness, clutching at his shoulders, moving her body urgently beneath his.

Suddenly her wrists were caught in the vice of his hands and Eve found herself forced back against the pillows. Shocked, she blinked up at the stone-faced, furious man who loomed above her.

'For God's sake, what is it that's so terrible you have to turn yourself into a tramp in order to stop me finding out?' Carl bit out fiercely.

Eve froze, the colour draining from her cheeks, leaving her pale and strained. She realised now that she had been right to be worried, for Carl had been pretending all the time. Desperately she sought a way out. 'I don't know what you mean,' she lied, and flinched when Carl swore.

'Don't take me for a fool! I knew when you walked in what you were doing. You're running scared, Eve, but what of and why? Tell me, you little fool, because you won't leave here until you do.'

One futile attempt to break free was all she needed to know she couldn't hope to fight him. She set her jaw. 'There's nothing to know. I came here to tell you I accepted your offer. I want fame and fortune, the good life. You said I could have them. I want you, too, and why shouldn't I have it all?'

Carl looked as if he wanted to shake her furiously. 'You're lying.'

'I'm not,' she denied, then went on tauntingly, 'You made the deal, and now you're backing out. Have I disappointed you? Did you think that because you were the first I was some sort of saint? Well, I'm not. I let my halo slip because you're a better proposition than Max. He's old, but I would have slept with him if he'd wanted. When there's something I want, I go for it. Now I want you.'

Carl had gone absolutely still as the sickening lies spilled from her lips. His face could have been carved from stone, so harsh and forbidding did it look. 'You're asking me to believe that?' he demanded coldly.

She met his look stoically. 'Yes.'

Eyes like blue ice-chips froze her in their contemptuous caress. He released her hands slowly. 'Then you'll know how to make it worth my while to give you what you want.' Thrusting the covers aside, Carl shifted on to his back. 'Show me just how grateful you'll be, Eve.'

Her heart stopped beating as a deathly cold spread out from the depths of her. Turning her head, she gasped at the sight of his beautiful male body spread out beside her. Nothing could be clearer than what he expected of her. He was challenging her declaration in the most basic way. If she was what she claimed, making love to him would be easy. Eve felt sick, knowing that she had driven herself into this trap and that there was no way out. She had to go on.

In disjointed movements she rose on to her elbow, and there was no way to stop her eyes from lifting to his. He was watching her impassively, coolly, leaving the choice up to her even as it dared her to continue. She found it impossible to hold that look, and dropped her gaze to where her hand rested on his tanned chest. It wavered as tears blurred her vision. If only he would meet her halfway, she could do this without the sick shame that knotted her stomach, but Carl wasn't about to help her. Telling herself not to think, she lowered her mouth to his shoulder.

For several minutes Carl lay impassive beneath her trembling caresses, then with a strangled oath he tangled one hand in her hair and jerked her head up. The muscles in his jaw flexed as he witnessed the glistening violet of her eyes.

'Damn you!' he ground out thickly, and thrust her away. In almost the same move he clambered from the bed, reaching for his robe and pulling it on, tying the belt with controlled violence. 'You'd go through with it, wouldn't you?' he charged, turning back to where she lay in a mortified heap.

Without another word, he picked her up. Eve couldn't struggle. All her strength seemed to have deserted her over the last few agonising minutes. Carl carried her from the room and down the passage to her own bedroom, his profile so rigidly controlled that she shivered. The light from her uncurtained windows showed him the bed and he strode to it, dropping her on to the covers ungently.

He stood there looking down at her dishevelled figure. 'Don't try that again,' he warned cuttingly.

Cold, her insides shrivelling before his anger, Eve met his eyes valiantly. 'You made the rules,' she whispered tautly.

There was murder in his gaze. 'Would it be so hard to trust me?' he bit out harshly.

'Yes!' Eve shot back, almost at the end of her tether. It wasn't a matter of trust. She couldn't reveal what wasn't hers to tell.

Carl's efforts to remain controlled were obvious, even in the half-light. 'I could kill you for the stunt you tried to pull tonight. It was cheap and unworthy. Just be thankful I had more pride than you, or you'd have had to go through with it,' he ground out through tight lips, then swung on his heel and headed for the door.

'What are you going to do?' Her anguished question halted him briefly in the doorway. He looked back.

'That I don't know. But believe me, when I do you'll be the first to know about it,' Carl returned with grim humour and left, closing the door abruptly.

'Oh, God!' Eve pressed her hands over her face as the tears that had burned her eyes and hurt her throat spilled over. It had all gone horribly wrong, and now Carl really despised her. But not as much as she despised herself. She had played cheap and felt it, and it made her love for him worthless. If he hadn't hated her before, he would now, and that hurt in a way she had never felt before.

With a convulsive sob, she rolled over, hands clutching the pillow that stifled her weeping as she gave in to her misery.

It was the hardest thing in the world to get up the next morning and face the others as if nothing had happened. She had slept—from sheer exhaustion—after that bout of weeping, but she didn't feel refreshed or rested.

Eve dreaded the first meeting with Carl, her nerves so stretched and fragile that she knew that one look or word of contempt from him would send her over the edge. But he wasn't at breakfast, and with relief she ate as much as her disappearing appetite would allow. By the time they did meet later, on set, Eve had been dressed and made-up, which gave her a shield of sorts. With any luck he would never witness the ravages caused by last night's fiasco.

Walking on to the set, Carl greeted her with cool formality, at once the single-minded director. Not by a look or word was their last meeting mentioned. It should have made her relax, but instead the studied politeness and lack of anything but professional interest chilled her. The result of last night couldn't be clearer. She had alienated him once and for all. While that was what she wanted, inside she was wretchedly unhappy. All she could do was summon up her composure and throw herself into the film.

There, too, things had changed. Used to hearing the order to retake, everyone was taken by surprise by Carl's clipped tones declaring, 'Print it.' The cast and crew were mystified, but relieved. Eve merely felt—abandoned. It was ridiculous, puerile, but she couldn't help it. She had never felt so alone and lonely in her life—and she knew in her heart that she would never be complete. For Carl had stolen a part of her she could never get back.

The unhappy pattern was set for the following days. With filming back to normal they gradually caught up with the schedule, and when Max returned, unheralded, they were actually creeping ahead. He arrived without warning, days later, and was simply there on the sidelines when they finished for the day. Eve, who had for once been a silent presence in the last scene, froze for an instant as her eyes met those penetrating grey ones. She had spoken to him only twice since that devastating conversation on her birthday, and as she forced her legs to carry her towards him that was what she was remembering now.

'My dear.' Max held his hands out, and she placed hers in them with a shiver. For an instant his eyes glittered, then with old-world gallantry he raised each hand in turn to his lips.

Aware that every eye in the room was on them, Eve pulled her tense lips into a smile of greeting. 'Welcome home, Max. I missed you.'

He smiled and his fingers closed tightly about hers, making her draw in a painful breath. 'Did you, my dear?' He released her, but only to turn her to face Carl who

had come across to them. 'So, my dear Carl, you progress, I see. And how has Eve been doing? Not *too* badly,
I hope.'

There was more to the question than met the eye, and
Eve held her breath as she saw the cynical twist of Carl's
lips.

'Shall we say, there's plenty of room for improvement, and leave it at that?' he stated smoothly.

'Ah,' Max smiled. 'So that was what Mrs Addison
meant. I wondered. With Eve so—busy—she's been
keeping me informed as to your...progress.'

Eve paled, but Carl merely looked interested. 'I've
noticed her—interest, but I should warn you that am-
ateurs have a rather uninformed idea of what is really
going on.'

'Naturally I bow to your superior knowledge,' Max
conceded smoothly, 'but now that I am here I trust you'll
indulge my wish to see the filming at first hand?'

Carl inclined his head. 'How could I refuse when
you've been so gracious as to allow us to use your home?'
he said drily.

'Thank you. And may my guest join me?' As both
Carl and Eve reflected their puzzlement, Max turned,
and they followed his outstretched arm to where, unseen,
a figure stood just inside the door. At Max's signal it
moved, revealing the stunning figure of a blue-eyed
blonde who barely looked out of her teens. 'Inge, let me
introduce you. Carl is the director of the film, and Eve
is...one of the stars. This delightful lady is Inge
Kaufmann. I'm hoping she will be staying with me for
quite some time.'

The blow was a deliberate, calculated cruelty. Eve
blanched, knowing exactly what was implied. By the
quality of the silence that descended, so did everyone in
the room. Those within her range of vision made a point
of not meeting her eyes. All except piercing blue ones
and they held hers without expression.

Yet no one quite knew exactly what was going on—
only herself and Max. Stiffening her spine, Eve held out
her hand to the disdainful younger woman, smiling as
best she might, determined to fight to the last.

'Welcome, Inge. I'm pleased to meet you. I'll have
Mrs Addison prepare a room for you.'

Inge's fingers barely touched hers before they were
withdrawn. 'That won't be necessary,' she replied
haughtily, in heavily accented English. 'Max arranged it
yesterday from New York.'

Eve's smile tightened. 'I see. Then you must let me
show you upstairs. I'm sure you'll want to relax before
dinner.'

Max intervened suavely. 'Don't trouble yourself, my
dear, you look tired too. It shall be my pleasure to show
Inge to the gold room. We shall all meet again, at dinner.'
With a comprehensive smile for the company, he steered
the leggy blonde from the room.

Eve watched them go, one hand raising to her throat,
feeling the frantic beat of her pulse there.

'So, what are you going to do now?'

Carl's cold voice made her jump and turn to raise
alarmed eyes to his face. 'What?'

He looked angry. 'Don't pretend you don't know she's
here as your replacement,' he goaded cuttingly.

Humiliated colour burned her cheeks. 'That has
nothing to do with you!' she snapped back in a choked
voice.

'Whatever use you may have been to him is over. God!
He's throwing you to the wolves!'

She knew that, but she was still here. There was still
a chance to retrieve the ground she had lost. 'Not yet,'
she responded gruffly, and was caught in a grip that made
her wince.

'What are you going to do?' Carl repeated harshly.

Eve, her face set with determination, was not really
listening, for she was too busy running over ideas in her

mind. 'Anything I have to,' she murmured grimly, not seeing the sudden tensing of his face.

'And if I don't let you?' he ground out.

She looked at him then in surprise. 'You can't stop me!' she retorted, then her face twisted bitterly as she looked away again. 'Why should you want to? I'm nothing to you. Just someone you wanted for a while—and had. Someone who can help you with your precious film! But there are other things in the world. Things that are precious to me.'

Carl held his breath for an instant, then said in a carefully level voice, 'Nothing is worth the sacrifice you intend.'

She met his eyes. 'Yes, it is. I've told you before not to interfere, and I'll say it again. Nothing is going to stop me. Not you—nothing.'

A nerve started to tick in his tightly clenched jaw. 'I don't believe that.'

Eve pulled away, tilting her chin defiantly. 'Watch me,' she advised caustically, and walked away.

CHAPTER NINE

WITH so much at stake, Eve pulled out all the stops. She had to believe there was a chance, that Max hadn't already decided to hand her over to the police. The trouble was that, now she had told him what he wanted to know, there was nothing to stop him doing exactly what he wanted.

She chose to wear the strapless black dress again, with the pearls. With her hair piled atop her head, the lustrous strands would be dramatically emphasised. One glance in the mirror reflected a dazzling figure, and she prayed Max would receive the message.

Eve shivered and lowered her lids, but it didn't help, for all she saw then was a pair of contemptuous blue eyes. Agitatedly she pushed herself to her feet. She must forget Carl, and all the pointless might-have-beens. She loved him, but he wasn't for her, so it really didn't matter what he thought of her—did it?

Oh, God, what a lie that was! She hated the thought of seeing the disgust return to his eyes. As it would, now that she had no choice.

Tonight, for the first time, Max didn't come to escort her down to dinner. She found out why as she entered the lounge and saw him already there, Inge clinging like a limpet to his arm. He saw her arrive, but made no move to join her or to invite her to his side. It was left to Carl to press a glass into her hand with a stony face.

'Still think you can do it?' he queried in an even, angry undertone.

Eve lifted her chin, but didn't meet his eyes as she brushed past him with a sibilant, 'Shut up!'

She went to talk to Harvey, and it was he who escorted her in to dinner when Max offered Inge his arm.

There was plenty of laughter during the meal, but it couldn't hide the tension in the air. Inge, seated at Max's right hand, preened under her host's almost undivided attention, and Eve sat at the end of the table, watching it all, with a cold, sick defeat taking hold of her stomach.

When Max raised the blonde's hand to his lips, Eve looked away, biting her lip. There was a fine tremor to her hands as she picked up her knife and fork, and she replaced them, dropping her hands into her lap lest anyone see. When she looked up, it was straight into Carl's blue gaze, and the controlled fury there told her that he, at least, had witnessed it.

Almost at the same moment Harvey launched into an amusing, not to say highly *risqué*, tale about a well-known star. As he addressed himself mainly to his host, Max was compelled to give him his full attention. The awful moment passed as laughter spread around the table. Eve joined in with a brittle gaiety, but Carl, apart from a thin smile as the tale finished, remained cold and withdrawn.

Enough to make Max turn his attention that way. 'My dear Carl, you're not enjoying yourself!' he exclaimed ruefully.

Carl sent Eve a piercing glance before regarding his host with a mocking curve of his lips. 'I have too much on my mind, I'm afraid.'

'I really cannot apologise enough about your film,' Max returned contritely. 'Is it completely hopeless?'

Carl drained the wine from his glass meditatively. 'I hope to be able to salvage something.'

'Now you make me regret my selfishness. Would it help if I insisted Eve withdraw?' Max offered, and there were few who would care to say his concern was false.

Yet Eve knew, and she drew in an audibly painful breath. Carl, however, didn't take his eyes off his opponent for a moment as he gave the suggestion due consideration.

'If we were at the beginning I would probably say yes, but at this stage there is no advantage to be gained. I'll carry on with Eve.'

Max spread his hands. 'I'm sure you know best, my dear Carl. It would seem I completely overestimated Eve's usefulness. Unusual for me, but these things happen.' He smiled apologetically.

Carl smiled too. 'We all make mistakes, even you, Max.'

The older man laughed. 'But never more than once. A lesson I learned early in life. After all, none of us is in the business of failure, are we?'

'No,' Carl agreed, glancing across to where Eve sat tensely waiting. 'None of us is.'

'Which reminds me of a story that will knock you out,' Harvey declared smoothly, and before anyone could object the mood had changed once again.

By the time dinner was over and they were once again in the lounge, Eve was wound up as tight as a drum, with a tense, nervous headache beginning to grow in strength at each passing minute. She was getting no-where, and knew she never would without Max's co-operation. He was playing with her, she knew that, but what she couldn't be sure of was which way he would choose to jump when the amusement began to wear off.

The couch dipped beside her, and she glanced round to find Harvey had taken the empty seat. She smiled. 'I want to thank you for smoothing over the rough patches tonight.'

The big actor patted her knee in an avuncular manner. 'Don't mention it. It was my pleasure. Besides, we were under orders.'

Eve opened her eyes wide. 'Orders?'

Harvey grinned. 'I probably shouldn't be telling you this, but what the heck? Carl warned us the going might be sticky for you. We all agreed to help if we could.'

Her lips parted on a surprised gasp. 'Carl did?' she queried faintly, eyes going to where he sat across the room talking to Nina.

'Um-hm. He's not an utter bastard, you know,' Harvey declared in amusement, and drew her gaze back to himself.

'I don't understand.'

'Evie,' Harvey sighed, 'if you came out of the wood, you might start to see the trees.'

'I can see his anger from right here,' she said heavily.

'Of course he's angry,' Harvey rejoined impatiently. 'But only because he cares.'

At that her eyes flew across the room again and encountered chilly blue ones. She shivered and looked away. 'You couldn't be more wrong,' she denied huskily. 'All he cares about is his film!'

'My lord, but you're stubborn, just like Colleen. My advice to you, Evie, is to remove the blinkers you're wearing, but soon.'

'Oh, Harvey, I——'

'Eve.'

She jumped as Max's soft voice interrupted from behind her. Stiffening, she turned to look up at him. 'Yes, Max?'

He held out his hand imperiously. 'My dear, you and I have things to discuss. I'm sure Harvey will excuse you. Come, my dear.'

Eve rose, placing her hand in his. The game was over. Now she was going to learn what came next. As she went out, she avoided looking at Carl, but she felt his eyes on her, burning into her back.

They went to the study. Max held the door for her to precede him into the room. She did so, her heart-rate accelerating as he entered and shut the door firmly behind him.

'Now, my dear Eve, I want you to sit down and tell me again just how badly the film is going,' he ordered silkily.

Pale and tense, Eve used the seconds it took to make herself comfortable to compose her thoughts. 'I've told you. I'm not an actress. Ask to see the rushes if you have any doubts,' she said, with the confidence of knowing they at least existed and would back her up.

Max took the seat opposite and crossed his legs. One hand tapped against the leather arm, the ruby ring on his finger glinting in the lamplight. Eve's eyes followed it, mesmerised, and something nagged at the back of her mind. His voice dispersed it.

'A little bird says differently. A little bird says you've been playing me for a fool. What have you to say to that?'

Faced with that, the only form of defence was attack. 'I'd say Mrs Addison is not only a jealous woman, but a liar,' she returned pointedly.

Max made a pyramid of his fingers and regarded her over them. 'The first is no doubt correct, but as to the second... She, at least, knows better than to lie to me. And you have been lying, haven't you, or why else did Inge's presence alarm you so greatly?' His hand slapped down hard on the chair arm, making her jump. 'I am not a fool, my dear, but I'm very much afraid you have been. I anticipated that Carl would tell you everything, but not that you would be foolish enough to agree to help him. That was a bad mistake. However, it can be rectified.'

Eve swallowed, trying to moisten a dry throat. 'How?'

Max smiled his crocodile smile. 'I have in my possession a sealed report—about you, my dear Eve. As yet it remains unopened. Call it a whim. It does, however, give me two options. To hand you over to the police and reveal whatever the report hides—or not. The latter depends on you. Reconsider your actions, and do what you were always meant to do. There remains half a film at least to sabotage. Your choice will govern my decision,' he finished reasonably.

Eve tightened her hands on the arms of her chair to hide their trembling. 'How do I know you won't do it anyway?' she asked thickly.

'Obviously you don't. You're a very foolish young woman. All you had to do was what I told you. You chose to disobey me, and I don't like that. You sought to trick me, and nobody gets away with it. I thought you were sensible. You knew the risks, yet you chose to flout me. Why? Why did you do it?'

Alarm turned her blood to ice. 'You know why.'

'Because you hate me? No, no, my dear, it's more than that. Something I didn't bargain on.' He paused then, and looked at her sharply. Suddenly grey eyes gleamed. 'My dear Eve, now that was really foolish of you. You've fallen in love with him!' His laughter held an unholy joy. 'Have you slept with him? I see. How delightful! But does Carl return the emotion? Somehow I doubt it. That whole family has a depressingly moral streak. It wouldn't stop him using you, though. However…having underestimated you once, it really would not be wise for me to do the same with Carl. It would appear we both have some thinking to do. I suggest you do so very carefully, and you have until the end of the week to reach the right decision. Now, we've deserted our guests long enough. Come, my dear.'

Eve went with him, obeying orders like a zombie. For the remainder of the evening, Max kept her firmly by his side. She was much too disturbed by his threats to feel the barbs of Inge's looks, or the worried glances of the others as they watched her strained features. She longed for the evening to be over, so that she could be alone to think. She was vitally aware of Carl's penetrating looks, but meeting his eyes was an impossibility.

She had hoped to avoid him altogether, but when Max went to replenish their drinks Carl was by her side in seconds.

'What the hell happened in there?' he demanded harshly.

She looked away. 'Nothing,' she lied, and his hand came out to clamp on her arm.

'Don't lie to me, Eve. A blind man could see something is wrong!' he exclaimed witheringly.

Feeling the shaking start deep inside her, she jerked back. 'I have a headache, if you must know, and you're just making it worse!' Why couldn't he simply leave her alone? Surely he could see that she couldn't take much more tonight?

Relief came from an unexpected source. Max came back. 'Talking shop?' he asked mildly, handing her her drink.

Carl's face emptied of all expression. 'I was merely reminding Eve she has an early call tomorrow. I'll knock on your door at six,' he declared thinly, and walked away.

When next Eve looked for him, he had gone. Everyone began to drift away soon after that, and Eve took the opportunity to go too. In her room, she swiftly showered and changed into her nightdress. Climbing into bed, she switched out the lamp and lay there, thinking.

She knew in her bones that even if she did what Max wanted—and what choice did she have?—he would double-cross her in the end. Yet a few more weeks would mean all the difference. Her mother was dying. If she could appease Max until then it wouldn't matter what he did.

The film would have to lose. She hated breaking her promise to Carl, but she just couldn't take the risk any more.

She thought of what Harvey had said, that Carl cared. She couldn't believe it. Yes, he had wanted her, but sex wasn't loving or caring, and that was all it had been for him. Besides, even that would die when he realised she was going back on her word.

Oh, God, how she wished it were all over.

Sheer nervous exhaustion made her sleep eventually, and so heavily that not even the slightest sound roused her.

Only a persistent knocking slowly penetrated, and she frowned. Groggily she rolled over on to her back, hearing but not recognising the door opening. However, Carl's voice brought her eyes open.

'Shake a leg, Eve, or we'll——' there was a sudden stop, then '—miss the light,' he finished stonily.

'My dear Carl, it's usually considered polite to wait to be invited in.' Max's voice from next to her drew Eve's head round sharply.

Her eyes dilated as she took in the sight of Max's pallid torso resting back against the pillows. Then, just as magnetically, her gaze flew back to the door. The violence on Carl's face made her blanch.

He didn't apologise, just remarked cuttingly, 'We begin filming in an hour. I'd appreciate Eve's presence in make-up in ten minutes. If you can spare her, *naturally*.' He underlined sarcastically and closed the door again sharply.

Max threw back the covers with a laugh and reached for his robe. 'And that takes care of any interference Mr Carl Ramsay may have been prepared to run. Some men are inordinately jealous where the women they sleep with are concerned. Carl strikes me as the sort who demands fidelity. His pride won't stomach what he just witnessed.' He turned to gaze down at Eve's stricken face. 'You have precisely five minutes to get ready. In the circumstances, I don't think it would be wise to keep Carl waiting.'

He left, and Eve closed her eyes. Dear lord, he hadn't missed a trick! How she loathed and despised him. And Carl—his face haunted her.

Twenty minutes later, washed and dressed, she presented herself downstairs. Pale, but with the stoicism of knowing that she had nothing to lose now. Carl was the only one in the morning-room, and he eyed her wan face with a tight, angry expression on his own. He didn't approach her, and appeared to be holding on to his temper by a whisker.

'You're late,' he informed her curtly.

'Sorry.'

He stared at her, a nerve ticking in his jaw. 'Is that it?'

She shrugged, body as tense as a bowstring. 'What else is there?'

Air exploded from between his teeth. 'You can't think of anything?'

'I didn't think you needed an explanation,' she returned tightly.

Carl's anger erupted spectacularly. 'My God! What is it going to take?' he demanded, crashing his fist on to the table. 'Are you just going to stand there and say nothing?'

'I know you're angry, but——'

'Angry?' he cut in incredulously. 'That doesn't come close to what I'm feeling right now! How could you let him——? I could thrash you, do you know that! With the greatest satisfaction. When I think of all that's happened! Hell! When are you going to wise up?' he growled fiercely, raking agitated hands through his hair. 'OK... You'd better get over to make-up before I give in to temptation.'

For Eve it was only the beginning of a long, miserable day. Although she tried hard to concentrate, she knew she wasn't at her best. There was only one consolation. When Max and Inge came to watch, they saw a much-below-par performance, which convinced him, if the gleam in his eye was anything to go by, that she had decided to toe the line. He at least went away satisfied.

Not so Carl. She was conscious of him watching her, the increasingly shuttered look on his face adding to her tension. Sometimes he looked as if he wanted to choke the very life out of her. If she needed proof that Harvey was wrong, she need look no further. He was making his dislike very clear.

Dinner was a tense affair, with Carl barely talking and Inge out to score what points she could. It amused Max, and Eve knew that Inge would be staying whatever happened. As Carl would so aptly put it, she was being replaced by a newer model. Well, as far as she was concerned, the German girl was welcome to him. So she swatted the barbs like flies and willed the evening to go quickly.

Carl excused himself immediately after dinner, taking Nina with him. They were gone for over an hour, and when they did return Nina's expression was troubled. By comparison, Eve encountered on Carl's face a new determination that made her catch her breath. It made her heart beat erratically as he made his way purposefully across the room to her.

'I've rearranged the shooting,' he stated without preamble. 'We'll be doing the scene with you and Dick tomorrow. There will be no need for an early start, but make-up would appreciate both of you having early nights tonight. Will you tell Max, or shall I?' he finished bluntly.

Eve paled and drew in her breath sharply. 'That wasn't very subtle,' she retorted coldly. 'Don't worry, I'll do any telling necessary.'

Carl produced a thin smile. 'Of course. Make-up at ten o'clock. Don't be late,' he ordered, before turning his back on her and joining the others.

She followed him with her eyes, hating him and loving him in a painful mixture of emotions. She decided then that she had had enough for one night. She was even prepared to argue with Max when she went to inform him she was retiring, but tonight he let her go without fuss. That brought a bitter smile to her lips as she made to leave.

At the door she glanced back, and regretted it as she met Carl's speculative gaze. He had witnessed the scene. Behind the cool mask of his face he was probably laughing at her. Damn him! Setting her jaw, she turned away, resisting with an effort the desire to rush madly to her room and cry out all her anguish into the pillows.

* * *

It was after ten the next morning when Eve left make-up and made her way back into the house to where a temporary wardrobe had been set up in one of the unused bedrooms. The scene they were to shoot was Velda Maxwell's seduction of the chauffeur, Jack Lloyd. Eve wasn't looking forward to it. She and Dick had only achieved a shaky truce over the last weeks. Sharing a bedroom scene with him, when she had never done one before, didn't make it easier to contemplate.

The wardrobe mistress gave her a cheerful smile when she walked in. 'I've laid your costume out behind that screen, Eve. You'd better hustle; Carl's been prowling already. Like a cat on hot bricks he is this morning.'

Another cause for her tension, Eve decided as she disappeared behind the screen. Stripping off her clothes, she reached for the flimsy covering. Expecting to find a matching nightdress and négligé, she found only the négligé. A brief scan of the floor showed her the nightdress hadn't fallen off the hanger.

'Doreen, you've forgotten the nightdress,' she called out.

'No, I haven't, honey. Carl's new instructions only mention the négligé, no nightdress,' came the answer.

Eve's heart thudded painfully. 'New instructions?' she queried unevenly.

'Sure. He gave me them as soon as I got here this morning. Is there anything wrong, honey?'

Stunned, Eve held the silky material to her. 'No,' she croaked through dry lips. 'No, nothing's wrong.'

But it was, terribly wrong. A coldness invaded her bloodstream as she recalled how Carl had looked last night. He had known then what he was going to do, how he was going to humiliate her and let her know exactly what he thought of her now. The depth of his contempt smote at her heart. How could he believe that she wouldn't care about playing the scene without clothes? It hurt so much that she couldn't even feel angry.

'Is Eve dressed yet?'

Carl's voice jolted along her nerves, bringing her head up. Dressed? Looking at the silky scrap of nothing, she bit back a hysterical sob. Dressed? Hastily she slipped it on, shivering at the coolness against her skin. With the négligé weighing nothing and hiding very little, she felt as if she were naked. There was a robe there too, and she put that on over the top before stepping out from behind the screen.

Carl was waiting by the door, looking relaxed in his usual jeans and shirt, but there was a peculiar sort of tension emitting from him that she picked up. He straightened and looked at her, the expression in his eyes a strange mixture of wariness and expectation.

'Ready?' he asked shortly.

No, she was not ready, and didn't think she ever would be, but she would not plead with him and call down more of his contempt. She would do this dreadful scene with what dignity she could. She would refuse to show him just how humiliated she felt by his deplorable actions.

She lifted her chin. 'Yes, I'm ready,' she returned coldly.

Carl's eyes narrowed. He seemed about to say something, then became aware of the hovering wardrobe mistress and thought better of it. His lips compressed into a thin line. 'You'd better come along, then,' he said abruptly, and led the way.

Shivering from nervous reaction, not the cold, Eve followed. The lights were on in the bedroom they were to use, for the windows had been blacked out to turn day into night. Dick was already there, dressed in a similar robe to her own. He gave her a mocking grin as she came in, eyes running over her speculatively. She couldn't stop the colour from storming into her cheeks and had the fleeting satisfaction of seeing the humour die from his eyes.

Then Carl was calling everyone to order. Save for the few technicians needed for the actual filming, everyone left the room. Then Carl began to give them directions.

Eve listened in mounting horror as she realised she was expected to discard the négligé entirely before climbing into the bed with Dick. However fleeting the moment might be, the thought of it was dreadful.

When Dick walked away to the bed, Carl turned to her. 'Any questions?' he queried, eyes boring into her ashen face.

She shuddered and abandoned her pride. 'I can't do it,' she declared huskily. She lifted her eyes to meet his, violet pools of anguish. 'How could you expect me to?'

A nerve started ticking in his jaw. 'How could I not? You've insisted all along that I see you the way you want me to. This is it. Are you telling me I'm wrong—after what I've seen, what I know?'

'Don't!' She swallowed painfully, and felt a pair of hard hands latch on to her shoulders.

Carl's face was alive with tension. 'If I'm wrong, Eve, then you'd better tell me. Tell me!' he insisted, shaking her.

'How could you?' she choked, too full of her misery to see beyond it.

Frustration and anger warred on his face as he let her go. 'OK, if that's all you have to say, let's not waste any more time.'

Her eyes dropped to the fastening of her robe as Carl moved off, giving orders in a voice tight and clipped. Trembling fingers released it and she slipped the robe off, taking care to keep the silky négligé covering her. She heard the instructions as if from a distance. The lights went out and silence fell. All she could hear was the agonised beat of her heart.

From somewhere she managed to dredge up enough acting ability to move from the door to the bed, discarding the wrap before slipping beneath the sheets as Carl had decreed, but it left her shaken and cold.

At her side, Dick gave her icy hand a reassuring squeeze. His voice, when he spoke, held a hitherto missing warmth. 'Relax, you're doing fine,' he told her.

Eve barely heard him. Her eyes were seeking Carl's glittering ones as he came over to give them directions for the love scene. He was so remote, so unemotional that a coldness settled inside her. When he walked away again, she realised that even now she had unconsciously been waiting for him to change his mind. He hadn't, and her agony deepened.

The next hour or two were a torment. Eve found an unexpected ally in Dick. He tried all he could to help her, but she couldn't relax. Each take was more wooden than the last. She couldn't bring down the mental shutters to distance her inner misery, nor find the ability to slip into Velda's character and forget her own. She was Eve Hunter, and Carl was tearing her apart.

When Carl called for a break, she lay back in silent despair, waiting for everyone to leave before she sat up and reached for the wrap. A movement drew her attention, and she turned towards the sound to discover that Carl hadn't gone, but was standing there, face hidden in shadows, watching her.

She dragged the sheet up under her arms. 'Why are you doing this?' she demanded in a low, pained voice.

'You know why,' he told her, moving forward and sitting down on the edge of the bed.

Eve looked away. 'Does it make you feel good?'

He shrugged, eyes never leaving her averted face. 'What do you think?'

There was the faintest gleam of anger in the eyes that met his. 'I think it's barbaric!'

Carl crossed his arms. 'When I want results, I use whatever method seems best.'

She gasped. 'Results? And if the method doesn't get them? What then?'

Blue eyes gleamed. 'I try something else,' he declared, hands reaching for her shoulders in a swift movement she couldn't avoid, bearing her back down on to the pillows. 'Like this,' he added throatily, and brought his mouth down on hers.

Shocked, she didn't fight, and after a second or two *couldn't* fight. Her senses swam as, after what felt like an aeon of drought, she received the storm of his lips and hands. Her arms went up around his neck, clinging as she returned his kisses, losing herself in them for one glorious moment. She was like quicksilver to his touch, expanding under the heat of his stroking fingers. As his lips left hers to travel her neck in search of her breasts, she arched into him, her breath coming in gasps from her parted lips.

'Remember, Eve,' he muttered against her warm flesh. 'Remember what it was like with us.'

She did, oh, so clearly. It had been magic. But magic had a darker side, and suddenly, unwanted, came the memory of what he had said, and the magic died. The suddenness of her arms pushing him away took him by surprise.

Violet eyes spat at him as she struggled to her feet and into her négligé. 'Why? So you can use it in your film?' she demanded hoarsely.

Carl sat up, a flush of colour dusting harshly set features. 'Is that what you really think?' he challenged sharply.

'What else is there?' she returned swiftly, angrily. She was so hurt and degraded, she shook with it.

Carl pushed himself to his feet, hands flattening down hair disturbed only seconds ago by her fingers. His face closed up. 'What else indeed?' he repeated flatly.

There wasn't a part of her that didn't ache as she glared at him. Her eyes were almost black. 'I hope God forgives you for that, Carl, because I never shall. Never!'

She fled then, on shaking legs, not to her room, but to the empty dressing-room, shutting the door behind her. Her hands flew to cover her disintegrating face. How could he? Oh, God, how could he do this? Easily, came the answer, and she shuddered. She had never felt so betrayed. It wasn't merely because of what he expected of her, but also that she had never believed he could do something so vile. It made a mockery of the person her foolish heart had begun to convince her that he was.

She truly hated him in that moment, and it was from that feeling that anger grew from a tiny spark. Carl might not know it, but he had just made the decision for her that Max demanded. She would do the scene exactly the way Carl wanted—but no more. He had destroyed her desire to help him at the same moment that he had defiled the memory of the beauty they had shared. She would give him what he wanted and shame the devil, even if she would never feel clean again.

By the time she arrived on the set again, Eve had encased her vulnerable heart in ice. Her face was pale, but set with a determination that wavered dismayingly when she encountered a pair of critical blue eyes. Only for a second, though, then she lifted her chin defiantly and saw his brows contract.

He crossed to her side and waited with barely concealed impatience while the make-up girl repaired the damages and then left. Thrusting his hands into the pockets of his jeans, Carl frowned at her.

'Changed your mind?' he challenged in a clipped voice.

'About what?' Eve returned shortly, and watched the clenched muscles in his jaw begin to tick.

'About the way I want the scene played,' he enlarged heavily.

Eve pressed her lips together to stop their trembling before she replied. 'No. Isn't acting supposed to draw from experience to make it more real? There's absolutely no reason why I shouldn't do the same!' she declared with all the control at her disposal, only walking past him when she felt it begin to slip.

The one word, 'Eve!', uttered in a tone she couldn't decipher had her turning back to him, totally unaware of the vulnerability in her violet eyes.

'Do you want this scene done or not?' she demanded to know belligerently.

Carl tensed, one hand rising to drag its way through his hair as he scowled. Then he squared his shoulders. 'OK, let's get on with it,' he ordered, in a voice that grated terribly on her nerves, because, like the idiot she knew herself to be, even now she was hoping he would change his mind.

It was too late for that now, and she took her place beside Dick in the bed, blanking out everything, willing herself into the character of Velda with a desperation that only partly succeeded. It gave to the scene that unfolded before the cameras a wildness future viewers would doubtless declare to be out-and-out lust, but which Eve knew was a growing reckless despair because she couldn't shut out reality completely. It was still her on the bed, not Velda, and when it was over she was left utterly drained.

Holding on at the very limits of her control, Eve sat up and reached for her robe. Her fingers trembled so badly they could scarcely function, and nausea was rising in her throat. Only when she was safely hidden from all eyes did she turn to Carl.

He was like a statue, pale and frozen, the look in his eyes condemnation of all that had passed. She gasped, her face crumpling in distress at this further confirmation of how little he thought of her. Her action was a compound of shame and hatred, and he must have known what she was going to do when her trembling legs brought her to him. Yet he made no move to avoid the palm that cracked against his cheek.

'Are you satisfied now?' she choked out, before turning and rushing away as the sickness rose. In her bathroom, the bout of sickness seemed to go on forever. It did end eventually, leaving her with only a desperate need to get away from the house, from everybody—and especially Carl.

With almost feverish haste, she cleaned her face and teeth, then dressed her shaking body in the first trousers and blouse that came to hand. Hair streaming, face bare of make-up, she fled downstairs and out of the front door. Only then did she realise she had no means of escape, and she could have screamed.

Her sob of despair turned to relief as she heard a car approach, and mere seconds later Nina turned her car into the curve of the drive, stopping level with Eve's distraught figure and climbing out fast.

'What's wrong?' she asked, face creased in concern.

Eve choked back a sound between a laugh and a sob. 'Oh, God, everything! Carl——' She stopped, unable to go on.

Nina didn't need to hear more. 'Oh, lord, I told him it wouldn't work!'

The muttered, revealing words went unheeded by Eve. 'I need your car!' she declared unevenly.

Nina hesitated uneasily. 'I really don't think you should drive in your state, Eve,' she argued, but found she couldn't withstand the unhappiness on the other girl's face. She stood back reluctantly. 'All right, but for God's sake drive carefully!' she cautioned anxiously.

Eve didn't wait for her to change her mind. Throwing Nina a grateful look, she jumped inside, selected first gear and put the car into a tight turn, never looking back. If she had, she might have seen Carl hurrying from the house, his frantic conversation with Nina, and then his lean figure running to his own car.

For Eve it was a wild, reckless drive, with no destination. Not knowing the country, she simply drove, mile after mile, out along the coastal highway, seeing nothing of the grandeur of the rocky coastline. The spectacular views out over the cliffs to the sparkling Atlantic passed by in a blur as she sought the unattainable.

How long it was before the truth finally dawned she had no way of knowing; all she did know was that she could never go fast enough, or far enough to escape her own despair. With that her foot eased on the accelerator, and finally she directed the car off the road on to a cliff-top vantage-point, and switched off the engine.

Climbing from the car, she walked across the grass to the edge of the cliff. The steep slope was rock-strewn, and many feet below the sparkling waters of the Atlantic boiled and surged against the rocky outcrops. The sound reached her on the breeze off the sea, lonely and mocking—an almost beautiful desolation. Sadness and misery surged up, but she blinked back the tears. It was over now, like all the other awful things she had faced, and if it hurt more than the rest, well...it would fade one day.

To her left an enormous boulder leaned out over the cliff, a natural look-out spot with a wide, flat top. Centuries of eager feet had worn foot holds on the weathered side, and Eve used them nimbly, standing tall on the surface. Looking out to sea, she felt as if there were only herself left in all the world. Four strides brought her to the edge and she peered down. The sight was breathtaking; she could see for miles either way, and down south—her heart ached—was the house, and Carl.

Away to her right she heard the sound of a car on gravel, then it stopped and a door slammed. Somehow, deep inside her, she just knew that when she turned it would be Carl she would see. She could almost feel his approach. It was uncanny, this feeling that her every atom was tuned to him and no one else. If she lost all of her senses, still the very essence of her would know him. She would never be free.

'Go away,' she commanded gruffly, without turning.

'Why? So that you can jump in private?' Carl demanded, with awful tension.

Eve looked up into the clear sky. 'I don't want you here.'

'That's too bad, because I'm staying,' he stated flatly, eyes carefully gauging the distance between them.

Angrily, her head swivelled to face him. 'This isn't a spectator sport!' she cried sarcastically, all the while noting his white, tense face and the coiled tension of his body.

A nerve ticked in his jaw. 'You know I'll try and stop you,' he retorted levelly.

Eve curled her lip. 'And risk going with me? This isn't a scene from one of your films, you know!'

'I'm aware of that,' he returned tautly. 'Nothing has ever seemed so real to me. Yet you'd better believe I'll try it. Where you go, I go.'

'"The grave's a fine and private place, but none I think do there embrace,"' she quoted harshly. 'Think what you'd be giving up in a hopeless cause.'

Blue eyes held hers by sheer will-power. 'I'd be giving up nothing. All that I hold precious would be gone with you,' Carl declared huskily.

Eve laughed. 'Oh, please, spare me this!' How dared he taunt her with such monstrous lies? 'After what you did to me today, I don't deserve it!'

The blood drained from his cheeks, but all that did was make his eyes burn with a feverish light. 'No, you deserve only the truth,' he agreed, his voice ever so faintly unsteady, revealing the strain he was under with the effort of stopping himself from doing or saying anything to precipitate her into the act he wanted to avert.

'The truth according to Carl Ramsay? There's nothing you could say that would stop me doing anything I wanted to do,' she scoffed, hitting back the only way she knew how.

'Yes,' Carl acknowledged heavily, almost to himself. 'It should come back to trust. I didn't have enough in myself and you have none in me. I should have gone with my instincts from the beginning.'

Violet eyes challenged him. 'What instinct was that? To condemn me out of hand?'

Carl shook his head solemnly. 'No, simply to love you.'

The sound of breakers far below faded away, so did the birds and the wind in the trees, as Eve stared at him, eyes wide and stricken. 'How can you say that?'

'Because it's true.'

He sounded so sincere that she started to crumble inside, wanting to believe this miracle, but so terribly afraid to. 'I don't believe you. You're only saying it so that I won't jump! You never gave any sign, not even...' She faltered on the memory of that afternoon on the beach. It was ridiculous to remember he had saved her life then too, as he thought he was now. 'Just when did this marvel occur?'

Carl stared up at her, so very aware of all her hurt, but knowing he must go slowly. There was a husky note in his voice as he said, 'That day on the beach was the most beautiful experience of my life. I should have told you then, because that was when I knew what I had always known, but hidden away. Eve, I fell in love with you that first night, when you were so proud and beautiful and ready to spit in the eye of those who thought themselves superior to you.'

Her lips started to tremble and she raised a hand to stop them. Her breath kept getting caught in her throat. 'You left me there,' she accused achingly.

Carl's eyes darkened. 'Darling, you told me you weren't free,' he told her softly.

Eve remembered that, and more. 'You hated me,' she declared, shuddering.

The truth he was committed to was painful to admit. 'Yes, I hated you. Because I thought the woman I had fallen in love with didn't exist. Couldn't exist, and be Max's mistress. What was I to think? You were so proud of it! At each turn you cast him in my face. Yes, I hated you, but not as much as I hated myself. Never had I been so wrong about anyone as I believed I was about you. Never had I been so hurt! No one had got to the very heart of me as you had. So I struck out at you like a child, because I was vulnerable and I couldn't let you see it. It was wrong, and I'm not proud of it. I don't ask you to excuse it, only to believe that it has been a very long time now since I hated you. There's no room, you see, because I love you, Eve, more than I thought it possible to love anyone. I know you're hurting, but don't take it out on yourself. You have far too much to live for. If you must hurt anyone, hurt me, darling, because I deserve it.'

The trembling had taken over her whole body now. She closed her eyes on tears of pain and sorrow—and a soaring sense of unbelievable happiness. 'I can't hurt you,' she returned brokenly.

Carl misunderstood. 'Oh, God, love, yes you can. So very easily, it's terrifying,' he declared thickly.

Eve gave a broken laugh and looked at him, scarcely able to see through the tears that overflowed. 'No, no. You don't understand. I can't hurt you because I love you.' She held out her hand to him. 'I've always loved you.'

Carl didn't seem to be able to move. 'Eve!' The ejaculation was hoarse.

She stumbled a step towards him, but her legs were so weak that she sank to her knees, laughing and crying by turns. 'Come and get me, because I don't think I can make it, and I need you so!'

CHAPTER TEN

WAVES crashed, birds sang, and Carl was with her atop the rock in an instant, dropping beside her and sweeping her into a bone-crushing grasp. Eve closed her eyes on a painful wave of happiness, clinging to him fiercely as he buried his face against her neck, muttering words she couldn't understand, but which her heart knew.

Reluctantly he let her go, kneeling before her to cup her cheeks in both his strong yet gentle hands and tip her face to his, scanning her eyes deeply, seeing there something that turned his eyes to the colour of the night sky.

'You mean it?' he breathed shakenly.

Amazed to discover her strong man needed re-assurance like everyone else, her face shone her love like a beacon. 'Yes.'

Carl closed his eyes. 'I don't deserve you.'

Her eyes softened. 'No,' she agreed, and his lids shot up at once in alarm, but, seeing her teasing look, he laughed unevenly.

'I love you. When I saw you up here...' He swallowed, unable to go on.

Eve lifted her hands to cover his. 'Carl, I wasn't going to jump. I only came up to look at the view,' she told him gently.

He stared at her. 'You only...?' She nodded at once, and he sighed raggedly. 'Dear God, and I thought I'd driven you to it with that damn stupid scene!'

Memory dulled her happiness. 'Why did you do it?' There was just no way to hide the hurt.

With a groan Carl pulled her close again, hands striving to soothe away the pain. 'Because you wouldn't trust me. You wouldn't let me in! God knows I tried.

That day I made love to you, I knew everything had been lies, and I came back from that swim determined to help you, but you refused to say anything.'

'You were angry,' she recalled, her words muffled against his neck.

'You're damn right I was angry. I knew Max, knew exactly what he was capable of. I was scared for you. I told you to trust me, but you wouldn't. God, I'd never felt so impotent. Every move I made failed. I wanted to help, needed to help, but without your co-operation I knew I was stymied. And you needed my help, so very badly.'

Eve groaned, seeing so clearly now. 'And that scene?' Instinct told her she had been wrong about that, too.

'Was a last, desperate attempt to get you to come to me. You were never meant to go through with it.' Carl gave a deep sigh, one hand stroking into her silken hair. 'I was scared for you when Max came back. I wanted to break every bone in his body for making you fear him. When he went so far as to let me see you in bed together, I was sure you would come to me then. When you didn't, I guess I went a little crazy.'

'You looked so angry, so contemptuous. And how could I ask you then? Max had guessed I loved you; he said you'd never want me now that he'd made love to me, too. But he hadn't, Carl. He never did!' She had to make him believe that.

'Shh. I know that. I loved you and I trusted you. It was Max I didn't trust. So I devised that scene. I'd seen your face when you tried to seduce me and put me off the scent. You hated it. If you couldn't be Velda then, you couldn't be Velda in that scene. You were supposed to back out and come to me. You'll never know how I longed for you to. Why in God's name did you go through with it? To punish me? Because, believe me, it did!'

Eve pulled away, seeing the hurt in his beautiful blue eyes. 'I went through with it out of pride. I couldn't let you see how much it hurt. I thought it was a—punishment. I didn't know you loved me.'

'Oh, God, what fools we've been! As God is my witness, I never meant to hurt you, Eve,' he swore softly.

She smiled. 'Nor I you.'

There were lines of strain about his eyes and mouth as he forced himself to say, 'Do you love me enough to trust me not to hurt you again?'

Eve frowned, searching his face. 'Of course.'

He smiled grimly. 'There is no "of course". Be sure, Eve, because I love you enough to give you your freedom if you want it.'

She lifted her fingers to his lips, eyes alight with love and moisture. 'Yes, I want my freedom,' she said softly, and when he moved violently away she pressed her lips quickly on his, so that he froze. She smiled at his bewilderment. 'I want my freedom, but there is no freedom without you. All the rest is an imprisonment of existence. Only your love can free me. When you make me yours, you give me everything the world can hold.'

The hands that drew her head to his for his kiss trembled. There was no passion in the kiss, yet it encompassed all the passionate intensity of the love they gave to one another. It took nothing, yet gave everything. A circle—complete. They were partners of the soul, and nothing time or distance could do to them would ever change it. This moment in time was all time.

Carl eased her away to look deeply into her eyes, revealing a love that scorched her. 'You are my soul, my light in the dark world. All of my future and what's good of my past. I love you.'

And out there, with only the wild beauty of Nature at her best as their witness, their vows sounded neither silly nor melodramatic. They might never say it again, but, once said, neither would forget it.

They smiled at each other, and only then did Eve realise they were still perched atop the rock. And that wasn't all.

'This rock is hard!' she complained, shifting her knees. 'Trust you to make a declaration of love in the most uncomfortable spot you could find!'

Carl rose nimbly and helped her up. 'Let me remind you, the choice was yours. I would have chosen somewhere softer, but fate had other plans,' he teased, as he climbed down to the ground and held up his arms to help her down.

Eve went into them without a qualm. Hands on his shoulders, she slid down the length of him in breathless provocation. Carl groaned.

'Right instinct—wrong time and place.'

'There's no one here,' Eve challenged, but lost her teasing when Carl's face sobered.

'Much as I want to take you up on it, we still have some talking to do.' He regarded her seriously. 'You know that, don't you?'

Of course she had known, she just hadn't wanted to bring back reality so soon. 'Yes, I know it. Carl, I know you want to help, but I honestly don't see how you can.'

'Neither do I—until you tell me. Or don't you trust me enough still?' he finished challengingly.

Eve gasped. 'Of course I do! It's just——'

'I know. It's been your fight for so long. But remember, you have me on your side now.' He sighed. 'Darling, tell me about your mother. She's still alive, isn't she?'

Fresh tears came to her eyes. 'Yes, but...oh, Carl, she's dying,' she cried, and buried her head against his broad shoulder.

'Tell me,' he urged, and this time she did. Carl listened in grim silence, not trusting himself to speak until she had finished. Only then did he say, in a voice cold as steel, 'It would give me the greatest pleasure to put my hands around his slimy neck and squeeze the life out of him. Failing that, we're going to beat him at his own game.'

Eve shivered, alarmed by the menace in his voice. 'How?'

Now Carl grinned down at her. 'I have the technology, and you, darling. All I need now is the help of a few friends I know, and the plan I have in mind will work like a dream.'

He was going too fast for her. 'Plan?'

'Sweetheart, we need to know two things: if the agreement still exists, and where it is. Max is going to tell us.'

She looked at him, aghast. 'Max is?'

Carl bent and pressed a swift, hard kiss to her startled lips. 'Mm-hm. Max expects you to give in—and you're going to. It will be your best performance to date. Grovel, and Max will love it. So much that he'll tell you anything. You and some friends of mine. Because, darling, you're going to be wired for sound.'

Eve lost her breath, catching on to Carl's enthusiasm. 'Will it work?' she asked breathlessly.

'You'll make it work. I know you can do it.'

There was only one thing bothering her. 'These friends—will I have to tell them everything?'

Carl knew at once what she meant. 'Only what they need to know. Your secret will be safe. Are you game?'

For a chance to beat Max? 'Try and stop me! But, Carl, what about you?'

'Me?'

Concern clouded her excitement. 'When Max realises, you'll have to leave. You'll lose your opportunity to find the evidence to clear Ruth.'

Carl's voice was gruff. 'Grandfather would have understood. In this you're more important.'

'I don't want you to give it up for me. I want to help you.'

'Darling, I love you for saying it, but my mind's made up. It was never really on. I had no idea what to look for or where. I set out to make a film and I will. I can do no more.'

Sadly she had to accept that Carl was right. 'So, what do we do now?'

'Now we drive in to Boston. There's no time to lose. Where did Max go today?' Carl asked, as he slipped an arm about her shoulders and steered her back to the car.

'He took Inge to New York. They'll be back for dinner.'

'Good. That gives us more time. You'd better lock Nina's car, we'll use mine. By tonight, I promise you, the nightmare will be over.'

Eve sat before her dressing-table putting the finishing touches to her make-up with hands that trembled faintly. The afternoon had been a whirl of activity. Carl had taken charge, getting a group of earnest people together, making her tell her story all over again except that part which involved her mother.

The outcome of it all was that she was sitting here, in a dress borrowed from wardrobe for the occasion, feeling more nervous than she had ever been in her life before. There was a tap at the door and she stood up, nervously smoothing down the narrow skirt, then raising her fingers to plump out the Spanish-style flounces about the neck and shoulders of the black and cream dress.

'Come in.'

It was Carl who entered, looking breathtakingly handsome in a dinner-jacket that moulded the male lines of his body. Smiling, he crossed to stand before her, scanning her features intently.

'Nervous?'

'A little.'

With gentle fingers he stroked the pale line of her cheek. 'You'll be fine. I have every faith in you.'

She twisted her head, catching his palm with her lips before gazing at him anxiously. 'What if——?'

His lips on hers stopped her, and sent all other thoughts flying, save the electrifying pleasure of his touch. He released her slowly.

'No what ifs. Max thinks he has you on the run. His conceit won't let him think otherwise. Just be brave for a little longer, darling, then I promise you I'll take you away from all this.'

Her smile grew in confidence. 'I can't wait.'

Another brief kiss and he headed for the door, pausing only to say, 'Remember, you're not alone. All of us here love you—but none as much as me. Break a leg, darling.'

She laughed, relaxing at the old superstition. 'I love you too, Carl,' she added softly, and turned to repair the damage to her lipstick.

Her confidence was fully restored as she descended the stairs later. She was into her role now, and knew she could carry it out. She had heard Max come in earlier, but he hadn't bothered her, much to her relief. Now all she had to do was follow Carl's plan and she need never fear Max again.

At the bottom of the stairs she paused, her right hand slipping under the flounces that fell to her waist, feeling the small box that was taped to her body. She hoped to God it was working, because she knew that one chance was all they had. Then she forced herself to banish the doubts. It would work. Lifting her chin, she forgot all but what she had to do.

Max was standing in his usual position by the fireplace, drink in hand, laughing indulgently at something the clinging German girl had said. The others were dispersed around the room, but they smiled at her when she came in, even Dick, and Eve realised that they knew and were rooting for her. For one silly moment she wanted to cry, but then she stiffened her spine. Her eyes flew to Carl's, seeing the blaze of emotion in his eyes that swelled her heart. Taking renewed courage from the nod he gave her, she walked over to stand before the dapper, grey-haired man.

'Max, I have to talk to you,' she declared, in a low voice that quavered at the edges.

He looked up at once, grey eyes penetrating. 'My dear Eve, can't it wait?'

Eve was aware of Inge's gloating look, but dismissed it. 'I don't think it can, Max. It's important. Please.' She twisted her hands anxiously.

At once Max was all attention. 'My dear, this isn't like you!' he exclaimed in concern. 'Naturally we can talk. In my study, I think. Please excuse us, everyone; we won't keep you long.'

Taking Eve by the arm, and ignoring Inge's petulant scowl, Max escorted her from the room and along to his study. The shutting of the door behind them sounded abnormally loud to Eve, and she moved forward into the room, collecting herself for the final confrontation.

'Now, my dear, what is it? Or can I guess?' Max sounded smugly pleased as he sat down, resting his hands on the carved arms of the chair like some middle-eastern potentate.

This was her cue. Turning, she paced back to the chair facing him, sitting down uneasily on the edge. She allowed herself one glance at him, then bowed her head.

'All right, you win,' she declared flatly.

'Ah!' Max's sigh was eloquent of satisfaction. 'How long I've waited to see that proud head bowed!' That brought her head up at once. 'But those eyes! You'd kill me if you could, wouldn't you, my dear? However, I'm glad you came to your senses.'

'I didn't have any choice, did I?' she declared huskily. 'That report . . .'

He smiled. 'Remains unopened—on your good behaviour.'

'So you won't hand me over to the police?' she asked, following the movement of his hand tapping against the armrest. As before, she saw the large ruby glitter in the light, the baroque setting adding to its grandeur. Something stirred in the reaches of her mind.

'Not yet.' Max drew her attention, breaking the link.

She licked her lips. 'That agreement, the one for the money, the one you denied. Where is it?'

Max chuckled. 'In a safe place. You need have no worries.'

She held her breath. 'So you do still have it?'

'Of course.'

Slowly Eve wiped her palms over her skirt. 'You may call me a fool, Max. I know I'm caught, but if I'm still to be blackmailed I'd at least like to know where the agreement is, to know it's safe. That I can have it when this is all over, as you promised.'

'Ah, yes. I did promise, didn't I? I shall keep my word. That unfortunate agreement still exists. It is safely locked up in the safety deposit box of my bank in Boston. You shall have both it and that report when I'm through with you. Are you satisfied?' he finished smoothly.

There, he had said it, and she sank back into her chair with relief. The small box beneath her breast weighed a ton, though it was weightless. Carl's plan had worked. Every word that they had spoken had been heard by a district attorney, a friend of Carl's, and the police. Already they would be acting upon the evidence. Now all she had to do was say the codeword and leave, allowing the authorities in to do their work.

Her lips parted, and as they did so she saw Max lift his hand, the one bearing the ring. Again that memory stirred. She had seen that ring before, but where...? Where?

The words remained unspoken. Instead she said, 'May I have a drink, please?' She needed time, time to flick through the album of her memory, seeking out the reference.

Certain of his victory, Max rose. 'Of course, my dear. And while we drink we can make plans for the downfall of Mr Carl Ramsay.'

He turned away, unaware that Carl's name had made the link. She had seen the ring with him. Seen it up-stairs, hidden away and forgotten in an attic. Seen it in a portrait, on the hand of a man who had died a violent death half a century ago. It was Henry Maxwell's ring! Her heart started to pound in her chest as she realised what she had done. She had found the evidence that Carl had come for.

It took all her efforts to remain calm, to act as if nothing had happened. Then, when Max returned with the drink, it was easy to take the glass and at the same time 'notice' the ring.

'Thank you. That's a fascinating ring,' she said evenly.

Max's free hand went to it in an automatic gesture, caressing it. 'Ah, yes, the ring. Do you like it?'

She nodded. 'It must be old.'

Max's lips twitched as he sat down again, inspecting the large ruby with satisfaction. 'Oh, it is. They call it the Borgia ring, you know. I doubt it's that old, but the allusion is intriguing.'

Eve moistened her lips, hoping against hope that somewhere not far away they were still listening. 'Yes, I can see it would be. Has it been in the family long?'

His teeth flashed. 'A very long time. I inherited it from my mother.'

'Your mother? You mean Velda?'

'This was her house.'

Eve puckered her brow. 'So it was, but I could swear I've seen the ring somewhere before.'

Narrowed eyes shot to her suspiciously, but she met them with an ingenuous gaze that relaxed him. 'I'm afraid you're mistaken, my dear. It's one of a kind.'

Eve's smile was an acknowledgement even as she frowned in mock concentration. 'And yet I could swear it. But if you say you got it from your mother——'

'It was her prize possession,' Max declared reminiscently.

'Was it really?' Eve murmured, something in her voice so different that it brought Max to attention, all the complacency gone in a flash. 'I'm not surprised. After all, she went to a lot of trouble to get it, didn't she?'

The look on his face was savage. 'What are you insinuating?'

She raised her eyebrows, 'Why, nothing!'

Max controlled the signs of a vicious temper with an effort. 'Then shall we drop the subject?'

Eve smiled. 'Of course, Max. Did you know I had a photographic memory?'

Max stood up angrily. 'My dear, you are trying my patience. I really wouldn't advise it.'

Eve rose too, gracefully. 'Do you remember everything you've put in the attics, Max? Do you, for instance, remember the two portraits of Ruth and Henry Maxwell?'

There was a very real fear on Max's face then, coupled with a deadly fury. 'Bitch!'

Eve's lips curled in distaste. 'You've been flaunting a dead man's ring under Carl's nose every day, haven't you, Max? Gloating in it. But you've overplayed your hand. You got too confident. You thought nobody would make the connection, but I did. You're wearing a ring that disappeared on the night of the murder and hasn't been seen since. Yes, you got it from your mother, the only way you could get it, because you weren't even born then. But how did she get it, Max? There's only one way—off her husband's finger—her murdered husband!'

She wasn't expecting him to fly at her with a swiftness that locked her limbs in shock. She screamed, and that triggered her reflexes to move. But she was a little late. As she ducked, one reaching hand caught her cheek, nails drawing weals, then she was stumbling over a stool and crashing to the ground. She pushed herself up in time to see Max reaching for her, face contorted.

'Bitch! I'll make you sorry you tricked me! I'll stop you from repeating those filthy lies!'

'Back off, Max, I've already heard them,' a formidable voice declared from the doorway, and they turned to see Carl framed there with the attorney and police flanking him. The latter pushed past him and manhandled Max away from Eve's fallen figure. Then Carl was on his knees beside her, lifting her shaking form into his arms. 'If you've hurt her, you bastard, you'll regret it.'

Max's grey eyes glittered wildly. 'You'll never be able to prove it. It's her word against mine!'

The district attorney moved forwards. 'Miss Hunter was wired for sound, Nilsson. We have everything on tape. I'll remind you that blackmail is an indictable offence. As for the rest, I think we'll start by taking that ring. We wouldn't want to lose the evidence for another fifty years, now would we? OK, officers, bring him along.'

Max was taken, protesting, from the room. Eve shuddered as Carl stood up with her. There was violence in his face as his eyes scanned her cheek.

'Can we please get out of here?' she said thickly.

Carl took the quickest way out, through the french windows on to the terrace. Eve dragged in the fresh, clean air, feeling the shaking gradually stop.

'It's over,' she declared flatly.

'There'll be a court case,' he advised her gently.

She shuddered. 'I suppose so,' she said, without enthusiasm.

'Darling, Max can't be allowed to get away with this. But we needn't discuss it now. Time enough for that later.' Taking a handkerchief from his pocket, he mopped up her face, lips thinned with anger.

'It's only a scratch. It will heal,' Eve assured him.

Blue eyes encountered hers. 'It was a brave, foolish thing you did tonight, but don't ever do that to me again. My nerves couldn't stand it,' he declared raggedly.

'Are you angry?'

Carl smiled ruefully. 'I probably will be when I get over being so damn scared!'

Eve slipped her arms around him, resting her head on his chest, hearing and delighting in the solid beat of his heart. 'I'm sorry, but I had to do it. Rolf was right. I'm so glad we proved it.'

'Grandfather would have been as proud of you as I am,' Carl muttered gruffly, then, 'Come on, let's walk down to the shore. I don't want to see this house again until we leave. The crew will be gone tonight, and so will we. Nina promised to pack your things.'

There was warmth still in the sun that was setting, and birds called in the trees that hid the house from view.

'I can scarcely believe it's really over,' Eve sighed, snuggling under the arm that held her so strongly.

'It is, well and truly.'

'And the film? We can't abandon it.'

One long finger tilted her chin. 'We won't. We'll finish it—after the honeymoon.'

'Honeymoon?' She smiled up at him coquettishly.

His lips dropped a swift kiss on her soft ones. 'You are going to marry me, aren't you?'

Her face said it all. 'Oh, yes,' she breathed softly.

'That's good, because your father's expecting us. He's arranging a small private ceremony in your mother's room,' he told her gently.

'Father is?' she repeated in blank surprise.

Carl nodded, smiling. 'I rang him with the news earlier. He said they would both be proud to be at our wedding.'

Eve's face crumpled in happiness and sadness. 'But she's so ill, Carl.'

One thumb wiped away her tears. 'But I know you'd want her to be there. And she'll know, darling. Believe me, she'll know.'

Yes, Eve truly believed that Colleen would know—in her heart. 'Oh, Carl, I do love you so!' she declared, so thankful that she had been given this man to love.

Carl drew her close into the haven of his arms. 'No more than I love you.' His hand stroked the silky fall of her hair. 'Always and forever.'

Harlequin Presents®

Coming Next Month

#1335 TOO STRONG TO DENY Emma Darcy
Elizabeth's principles lead her to ask Price Domenico, a top lawyer, to clear her
of something she hasn't done. She needs his help no matter what it costs,
though she hadn't reckoned on it costing her heart....

#1336 LOVE AT FIRST SIGHT Sandra Field
Bryden Moore is blind, but Casey Landrigan knows his real problem is his
inability to love. Neither denies the growing attraction between them, but do
they stand a chance when Bryden discovers Casey's true identity and the real
reason she's vacationing next door?

#1337 WEB OF DESIRE Rachel Ford
The request to go to the Caribbean island of Halcyon Cay to restore valuable
tapestries should have delighted Camilla. Instead it throws her into turmoil.
For Halcyon Cay would have been *her* island if it weren't for Matthew Corrigan.

#1338 BITTER SECRET Carol Gregor
The charismatic new owner of Sedbury Hall is an unwelcome intrusion into
Sophie's well-controlled world. She's instantly attracted to him—but
determined to live her life alone....

#1339 TIME FOR TRUST Penny Jordan
The traumas of Jessica's past mean she can no longer trust anyone—not even
her parents. Then she falls in love with and weds Daniel Hayward—but would
love, without trust, survive?

#1340 LET FATE DECIDE Annabel Murray
It's easy for Jenni to believe that meeting Clay Cunningham's blue eyes across
a crowded marketplace was meant to happen. But it's not so easy for Jenni to
cope with her feelings once Clay makes it clear that any relationship between
the two will be on his terms.

#1341 THE DEVIL'S EDEN Elizabeth Power
Coralie Rhodes—working under the name Lee Roman—desperately needs an
interview with Jordan Colyer's famous uncle, to rescue her flagging magazine.
But events of eight years ago had convinced Jordan that Coralie is a gold
digger. Will he take his revenge now?

#1342 CONDITIONAL SURRENDER Wendy Prentice
Kate is shocked when Greg Courtney, her boss, reveals he's been burning with
desire for her since their first meeting. Kate finds him attractive,too, but Greg
is a cynic who doesn't believe in love. Kate is a romantic and knows that
it's essential.

Available in February wherever paperback books are sold, or through
Harlequin Reader Service:

In the U.S.
901 Fuhrmann Blvd.
P.O. Box 1397
Buffalo, N.Y. 14240-1397

In Canada
P.O. Box 603
Fort Erie, Ontario
L2A 5X3

You'll flip . . . your pages won't!
Read paperbacks *hands-free* with

Book Mate · I

The perfect "mate" for all your romance paperbacks
**Traveling • Vacationing • At Work • In Bed • Studying
• Cooking • Eating**

Perfect size for all standard paperbacks, this wonderful invention makes reading a pure pleasure! Ingenious design holds paperback books OPEN and FLAT so even wind can't ruffle pages — leaves your hands free to do other things. Reinforced, wipe-clean vinyl-covered holder flexes to let you turn pages without undoing the strap . . . supports paperbacks so well, they have the strength of hardcovers!

Pages turn WITHOUT opening the strap.

SEE-THROUGH STRAP

Reinforced back stays flat.

Built in bookmark

BOOK MARK

BACK COVER HOLDING STRIP

10" x 7¼", opened.
Snaps closed for easy carrying, too.

Available now. Send your name, address, and zip code, along with a check or money order for just $5.95 + .75¢ for delivery (for a total of $6.70) payable to Reader Service to:

Reader Service
Bookmate Offer
3010 Walden Avenue
P.O. Box 1396
Buffalo, N.Y. 14269-1396

Offer not available in Canada
*New York residents add appropriate sales tax.

BM-GR

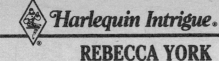

Harlequin Intrigue®

REBECCA YORK

Labeled a "true master of intrigue" by *Rave Reviews*, best-selling author Rebecca York makes her Harlequin Intrigue debut with an exciting suspenseful new series.

It looks like a charming old building near the renovated Baltimore waterfront, but inside 43 Light Street lurks danger . . . and romance.

Let Rebecca York introduce you to:

> *Abby Franklin*—a psychologist who risks everything to save a tough adventurer determined to find the truth about his sister's death. . . .
>
> *Jo O'Malley*—a private detective who finds herself matching wits with a serial killer who makes her his next target. . . .
>
> *Laura Roswell*—a lawyer whose inherited share in a development deal lands her in the middle of a murder. And she's the chief suspect. . . .

These are just a few of the occupants of 43 Light Street you'll meet in Harlequin Intrigue's new ongoing series. Don't miss any of the 43 LIGHT STREET books, beginning with #143 LIFE LINE.

And watch for future LIGHT STREET titles, including #155 SHATTERED VOWS (February 1991) and #167 WHISPERS IN THE NIGHT (August 1991).

HI-143-1